## ONCE UPON A TIME . . .

From the depths of night, out of rain and fog, like a demon rising from the smoke of Hades, a magnificent black stallion swirled into the bit of light that dwindled down from the two windows at the top of the slender tower. The beast reared and snorted and pawed at the air. As it settled, a slight figure in a wildly billowing cloak jumped to the ground and gazed upward. Amidst a rising wind and flashing lightning and a teeth-rattling clap of thunder, a distinctly feminine voice called upward. "Rapunzel! Rapunzel, let down your hair!"

What the deuce? thought Sir George confusedly, and then his weary emerald eyes opened wide. "By Jove!" he gasped.

From one of the tower windows a braid of golden hair tumbled to the ground below. The figure in the billowing cloak seized one handful after another of that marvelous braid and scurried up it, leaping, at the last, nimbly in through one of the windows.

"Jupiter!" exclaimed Sir George under his breath. "Jupiter!"

# Once Upon A Time

*Carola Dunn*

*Karla Hocker*

*Judith A. Lansdowne*

Zebra Books
Kensington Publishing Corp.
http://www.zebrabooks.com

ZEBRA BOOKS are published by

Kensington Publishing Corp.
850 Third Avenue
New York, NY 10022

First Printing: September, 1998
10 9 8 7 6 5 4 3 2 1

Printed in the United States of America

# Contents

# Rumplestiltskin

# Chapter One

"Mother?"

The slight young man scanned the still surface of the ornamental lake. Ringed by yellowing reeds, it reflected the cold steel-grey of the twilight sky. In spite of top-boots and buckskin riding breeches, his lame leg ached with the chilly dampness.

"Mother!" he called again.

A rustle among the reeds preceded the appearance of a sleek brown head. Dark, intelligent eyes questioned him.

"Tell Mother I'm here."

The otter whistled and slid into the water. Spreading ripples lapped at the reeds. Edward waited.

Not for the first time, he wished his mother would remove into the house for the winter. She swore she felt warmer at the bottom of the lake, whither she had retired when her beloved husband died, but it was deuced uncomfortable for Edward when he wanted to talk to her.

At least the concealing woods kept off the biting wind.

Smoothly silent as a trout rising to a fly, Daphne, Baroness Tarnholm, ascended from the depths, spangled with silvery drops. Green-gold hair, slanted eyes the green of water-worn bottle glass, a piquant face with pointed chin, slender white shoulders, small, high breasts . . .

*"Mother!"*

"Oops, sorry, dear."

Her ladyship ducked, to reemerge a moment later with the offending portions of her anatomy covered by two tiny scraps of fabric, purple spotted with yellow.

"Good Lord, what is that?" asked her son, stunned.

She glanced down at her front. "It's my itsy bitsy teeny weeny yellow polka dot bikini," she said with pride, then added sadly as she saw his blank expression, "Drat, wrong century."

Ducking again, she came up draped in a swansdown shawl. "There we are. Now we can talk without you getting all hot and bothered."

"I could do with some heat."

She gestured at him with slightly webbed fingers and at once a gentle warmth seeped through him, easing the pain in his leg. The sodden wood of the nearby bench lightened as it dried with magical speed. "Sit down, dear, and tell me what's going on."

"Reggie's coming home, Mother, and it is all my fault," he told her gloomily. "I wrote to him to point out that Cousin Lizzie will be eighteen next month and she really ought to make her bow to Society come spring."

"That's bringing the duke home? After five years of utterly ignoring the existence of his sisters?"

"He writes that a friend of his pointed out to him that if he doesn't marry them off, he'll have them on his hands forever."

"On your hands, Edward. Who has overseen their

upbringing since your dear father died? Not the noble Duke of Diss. Though I cannot altogether blame
him; last time I saw them, I decided a more shockingly insipid troop of young ladies doesn't exist. They
take after their mother. Alicia never had an ounce of
gumption."

"I'm fond of my aunt," he protested, "and of my
cousins, too. By the way, it's past time you came up
to the house and entertained them to tea. It's all very
well being thought an eccentric recluse, but if you
are never seen I shall be suspected of doing away with
you."

"Nonsense, the duchess knows very well what I
am."

"For thirty years she has managed to persuade herself that she imagined the debacle of my christening."

"Oh, very well. Arrange a date and I'll struggle into
my crinoline. . . . No? Thank heaven for small mer-
cies! Of all the simply frightful fashions, only the Gre-
cian bend is . . . was . . . will be worse. I do get a bit
confused about time, living down here," Lady Tarnholm admitted.

"I shall check what you are wearing before you appear in the drawing room. How we should manage
without loyal and discreet servants I cannot imagine."

"They are quite as fond of you as they were of your
father, dear."

"And of you, Mama, on the rare occasions they see
you. Anyway, as I was about to say, my chief concern
is not for my cousins. Reggie cannot get his sticky
hands on their dowries, and they are all pretty
enough, besides being sisters of a duke. They will find

husbands whether or not I can persuade him to sport the blunt for their Seasons."

"Then what has got your knickers in a twist?"

"What has *what*?! Never mind, I can guess. I'm worried about the maidservants and farmers' daughters. You know Reggie's disgraceful reputation."

"I shouldn't worry, dear. Country innocents have never appealed to him in the least. He'll not spare a second glance for dairymaids in stuff gowns and pattens or tweenies in caps and aprons."

"Tweenies?"

"In-between maids. An unhappy and downtrodden cross between a housemaid and a scullerymaid. You don't have any?"

"Not to my knowledge," said Edward dryly. "I trust none of my servants is downtrodden."

His mother concentrated, the lightest of frowns wrinkling her smooth, white forehead. "Ah, late Victorian, I believe. Sixty or seventy years hence. No, Reginald wouldn't care for tweenies. He's too frightfully like his father for words. It's the bejeweled and painted Birds of Paradise in their silks and satins he fancies."

Edward sighed. Just as the fashionable Cyprians of London used their fine attire to attract protectors, he could, if he chose, use his title and fortune to win a bride. But he didn't want a wife who had married him for the sake of her own or her parents' ambition.

He wanted to be loved. Yet what woman could love a man with a limp, with one shoulder a smidgeon higher than the other, with fox-red hair, eyes of a curious silvery grey, and a face that missed ugliness by a hairsbreadth? Add his small, fine-boned stature and it was no wonder the villagers regarded him as a changeling.

Old Mrs. Stewart was drowsing in her rocking chair, her snowy cap resting against the back, mittened hands folded in her lap. With a sigh of regret, Martha marked the place in Miss Maria Edgeworth's *Tales of Real Life* with a leather bookmark and set the volume on the table.

After tucking the pink shawl securely around the old lady's shoulders, her rug about her black bombazine knees, Martha poked up the fire before she took her money from the table. She loved reading aloud to the vicar's aged mother. Mam did not mind, because young Mrs. Stewart paid her as much for her time as she would get for sewing.

The vicar's wife—fifty if she was a day but still young Mrs. Stewart to the villagers—was passing through the front hall when Martha stepped out of the old lady's room.

"She's asleep, madam," Martha said, bobbing a curtsy.

"She always sleeps well after you have read to her, Martha. She does enjoy it so. You read very well."

"It's thanks to you I can read at all, madam, and write. And I enjoy it, too. If it wasn't for this job, I'd never have a chance. I'll be away home now if there's naught else you want me to do while I'm here."

"There is something. Just a moment." Frowning in thought, Mrs. Stewart continued absently, "You have an excellent speaking voice, also, not at all common as one would expect of a miller's daughter."

"Thanks to Mrs. Ballantine, madam. Whenever I

go to sew for her young ladies at the Academy, I'm allowed to listen to their lessons," Martha explained patiently, not for the first time. Young Mrs. Stewart was renowned for her forgetfulness.

"Sew!" she exclaimed. "That is it. I tore the lace on my Sunday best grey silk, and no one can do invisible mending as well as you can, my dear."

Martha much preferred creating new gowns to mending old, but with eight younger brothers and sisters to be fed, any kind of work was not to be turned down. Her tiny, neat stitches soon fixed the rent to Mrs. Stewart's satisfaction.

She left the vicarage with an extra sixpence jingling in the pocket of her old blue woollen cloak. Walking homeward past the church and through the village, she cheerfully hummed the old ballad of "John Barleycorn."

" 'They ploughed, they sowed, they harrowed him in,

" 'Throwed clods upon his head.

" 'And those three men made a solemn vow,

" 'John Barleycorn was dead.' "

In the gardens of the reed-thatched, whitewashed wattle and daub cottages, nothing grew but Christmas roses, snowdrops, and cabbages. It was a mild day for January, though, and Martha threw back the hood of her cloak. On a day like this, spring seemed not so very far away.

" 'Then they let him lie the winter through,

" 'Till the rain from heaven did fall.

" 'Then little Sir John sprung up his head,

" 'And soon amazed them all.' "

As she passed the Pig and Peasant at the crossroads, Tad, the landlord's son, dashed out.

"Martha," he cried, "I bin watching for you. You going home? I'll walk a ways wi' you."

She tossed her golden curls and said, "Who invited you?" but she smiled. Tad was a likely lad, strong as an ox with his thatch of straw-colored hair and merry eyes.

"Aw, Martha, you know you be agoing to marry me in the end."

"That I'm not! Or maybe I am, but not for ages yet. If Lady Elizabeth goes off to London-town come spring, I want to go along as her abigail."

"Aw, Martha, I can't wait that long!"

"If you can't, there are plenty who will," she assured him, cornflower-blue eyes flashing.

"There's not so many as has a good living waiting for 'em like I has at the Pig."

"What if the duke was to decide to rent the inn to someone else?" Martha teased.

"Why would he? 'Sides, long as he gets his rent his Grace don't care a button who's landlord o' the Pig, off raking in London as he is. He ain't bin near Willow Cross in going on five year."

"I can't remember when he was here last," she conceded.

"Lord Tarnholm's the one as says what goes," Tad persisted, "and he's fair for all he's a changeling. He wouldn't turn anyone out for nowt. So Lady Elizabeth's really going to London, is she?"

Martha shrugged. "She's eighteen. It's time for her to make her curtsy to the poor old Queen and go to fancy balls and such, looking for a proper husband. But it all depends whether the duke remembers she exists."

"He don't take no more account o' his family nor he don't o' his tenants," Tad agreed.

Reaching the humpbacked bridge over the stream by the mill, they stopped to lean on the stone parapet and watch the swirling waters below. The usually placid brook was swollen with winter rains, its roar competing with the familiar creaking rumble of the great mill sails. Above the din, Martha heard the thunder of galloping hooves.

Round the bend of the lane on the other side of the stream sped a coach and four.

Martha and Tad scrambled out of the way as the top-hatted coachman, huge in his multi-caped great-coat, reined in his team to cross the narrow bridge. The matched blacks were lathered with white froth from their wild course. On the door panel of the royal-blue carriage a ducal crest was picked out in gold. Through the window, Martha caught a glimpse of a darkly handsome, arrogant face within, before the coachman whipped up the horses again.

"Looks like he 'membered his sister arter all," Tad observed, staring disconsolately back down the village street after the racing carriage with the two footmen clinging on behind. "And a right hurry he's in. Let's hope he don't start poking his nose in and interfering wi' the rest on us, for we go on mighty well wi'out his Grace."

Martha nodded, said goodbye, and went on to the mill house with her head in the clouds. Never in all her born days had she seen such a splendid, dashing gentleman.

"The duke's come home," she told her mother, a plump, grey-haired, harried woman with a child on her hip and another clinging to her skirts. "He's ever so handsome."

"Handsome is as handsome does," Mam grunted, stirring the savoury-smelling soup in the kettle hanging over the fire, "and by all accounts his Grace ain't one to put hissel' out for nobody. It's to be hoped he don't upset things as is running smooth without him. Take your cloak off now, Martha, and cut some bread and bacon for supper."

Dreamily, Martha obeyed. A duke was something special, she thought. You could not judge him by the same standards as ordinary people.

# Chapter Two

"I'll be damned if I'm going to spend the morning conning account books," said the Duke of Diss petulantly, pushing the heavy volumes aside. "To the devil with 'em, say I! I suppose I can count on my own cousin to keep my bailiff honest, and if he's not, you have my permission to kick the good-for-nothing out and hire another."

"I believe him to be an excellent man," Edward assured him, "but I have my own estate to oversee."

"Pooh, your place is too small to take up much of your time, and I wager you don't aspire to cut a figure in Town."

"Which is why I cannot bring out Lizzie for you."

"Oh, I don't mind squiring her to a few parties, now I've seen she's at least halfway presentable. Not butter-toothed nor squint-eyed, thank heaven! But I daresay it's going to cost me a small fortune to fig her out for the Season. And five more to go! I'd forgot I have so devilish many sisters."

His dark brows meeting in a scowl, he stood up, towering over his cousin. He was dressed in a brown shooting jacket, fawn buckskins, and tasselled top-boots, so it was no surprise when he announced, "I'm off to bag a few pheasants."

"A few is all you'll find," said Edward, not without a certain relish. "I haven't had your coverts kept up as you are never here."

"Ducks, then. Or have you drained the North Marsh?" Reggie asked suspiciously.

"No, you will find plenty of waterfowl and snipe there, but you scarcely have time to go so far. Your principal tenants will be here at noon."

"To hell with my tenants! I've nothing to say to 'em, damn their impudence."

"*I* arranged the audience," Edward said dryly, "and not at their request. I felt it to be only proper that they seize this rare opportunity to offer their obeisance. Come, Cousin, you surely will not forego a chance to dazzle them with your noble condescension?"

The prosperous farmers, the miller, and the innkeeper knew better than to consult the duke about any matter of substance. In fact, Edward had not found it easy to persuade the reluctant men that they ought to pay their respects to their absentee landlord.

"Oh, very well," Reggie conceded, with a trace of sulkiness belied by the light in his eyes. "The new blue morning coat from Weston, I think, and my neckcloth tied in the Mathematical, with the diamond pin. I'll see what my man suggests in the way of a waistcoat." His broad shoulders squared to meet the challenge of impressing the peasants, the duke strode from the room.

Just what went on beneath those fashionably coiffed dark locks? Edward wondered. On the whole, he decided, he'd rather not know.

The Mathematical knot proving troublesome, his Grace kept his tenants waiting in the Tudor great hall for the better part of an hour. Stiffly dressed in their Sunday best, they pretended to examine the faded armorial bearings, or eyed the minstrels' gallery and the high hammerbeam ceiling with knowledgeable mutters of "dry rot."

To Edward's amusement, two of the farmers engaged him in a discussion about the possibility of draining the North Marsh, at the far end of the estate. He had to agree that it could provide a goodly acreage of excellent pasture. Let his Grace stay away another five years, he told them, and he would consider allowing the drainage.

They abandoned him forthwith when the duke descended the age-blackened, carved oak staircase. Even his disaffected cousin had to admit he made a magnificent entrance.

The great tailor Weston's coat fitted him like a glove, as did his dove-grey inexpressibles. His refulgent Hussar boots shone scarcely less than the gold fobs at his waist and the gold brocade waistcoat that a stickler might have considered more suited to a ballroom. In the elaborate folds of his pristine neckcloth glittered a large diamond. His tall, elegant figure moved with a studied grace, and the expression on his patrician face was one of haughty disdain. Lip curled, he raised his quizzing glass.

Awed, the tenants moved together for support. Edward introduced them one by one. Reggie greeted and dismissed each with a gracious nod and a word or two. None ventured to do more than express his utmost respect until at last it came to Tom Miller's turn.

"If it please your Grace," he blurted out, "I've a daughter."

The duke raised supercilious eyebrows.

"She's a good lass and a pretty un, your Grace," the stout miller stammered, "and she'd like fine to be abigail to her ladyship Lady Elizabeth, your Grace."

"Indeed," said Reggie coldly.

Edward was ready to intervene before he gave the poor fellow a shattering set-down, or even dismissed him for his impertinence. But Tom, his always ruddy face redder than ever, was determined to do his best for his daughter and he rushed onward.

"My Martha's the best seamstress in the county, your Grace. Why, she can turn a scrap o' muslin into a ball gown fit for a duchess, quick as winking."

Reggie's attention was well and truly caught. "She can, eh? Lady Elizabeth's going to need a whole new wardrobe for London. I suppose the girl could manage that in a day or two?"

"Oh yes, your Grace, sure as eggs is eggs, and better nor any London dressmaker," Tom boasted. "Everyone says so."

"Send her up to the house tomorrow noon, my good man, and we shall see what she can do."

"Yes, your Grace. Thank you, your Grace." The miller went off looking pleased with himself.

Equally pleased with himself, Reggie turned to Edward. "This will save me a pretty penny. You wouldn't believe what the fashionable London modistes charge."

"You shouldn't believe Tom Miller's bragging," said Edward. "He's famous for his tall tales, and his tongue tends to run away with him."

His cousin frowned ominously. "You mean he's not

telling the truth? The girl can't sew? By gad, he'll suffer if he's lied to me."

"Martha can sew, most beautifully, I understand. In fact she already makes some of your sisters' clothes. But I suspect Miller's vision of a fashionable London wardrobe is two or three round dresses and a ball gown."

"Devil take it, I'm not such a credulous slowtop as you think," said the duke, annoyed. "I daresay it may take her several days to make all Lizzie needs. But if she is as good as he says, I shall save a small fortune I have much better uses for. Tell Lizzie to make up her mind exactly what she wants, will you, coz? I'm going duck hunting."

He dashed off up the stairs much faster than Edward, still protesting, could limp after him.


Martha wanted to skip as she made her way to the great house at midday next day. Though she restrained herself—skipping was beneath the dignity of an abigail-to-be—excitement bubbled within her.

She touched the lucky four-leaf clover in her pocket, that she had found last summer. She was going to see London, and with her expenses paid so that all her wages could go to her parents. She was going to be living in the same house as the magnificent duke. Pa had told them what a splendid figure he made, dressed up to the nines, tall and handsome and haughty.

Even Mam had grudgingly agreed it was good of his Grace to give Martha a chance to display her abilities.

Of course she knew better than to expect a great nobleman like the Duke of Diss to pay his sister's maid the least notice, but she was bound to catch a glimpse now and then. Dreaming was free, wasn't it?

She had no doubt of her ability to create an elegant wardrobe for Lady Elizabeth. The local gentry always sent for Martha Miller and her clever needle when they needed a special gown for the assemblies in Newmarket or Bury St. Edmunds.

As she passed a poplar windbreak, the tall, narrow trees leafless now, she paused to admire the mansion. With its grey stone towers and turrets, imposing gatehouse and crenellated walls, it reminded her of a woodcut of a king's palace in a book of faerie stories she had once read to old Mrs. Stewart. A fitting home for the splendid Duke of Diss.

Walking round to the servants' entrance in the east wing, Martha turned her mind to the task ahead of her. Silks, satins, and velvets she would be sewing, instead of the winter flannels and worsteds and the summer muslins she was more accustomed to. Rich lace by the ell, fur trimmings for pelisses, gold and silver thread embroidery—the young ladies had shown her pictures in the London magazines. If she did a good job, perhaps his Grace might smile at her?

Mrs. Girdle, the housekeeper, who was Tad's auntie, met her with a worried face.

"I hope you haven't gone and bit off more than you can chew, Martha." She led the way up a winding stone staircase to the sewing room, high in one of the towers. "His Grace gets some mighty odd notions into his noddle, there's no denying, and what with your pa's getting carried away by his own tongue the way he does. . . ."

"Why, I'll just have to do the best I can, ma'am,"

said Martha gaily. "If I don't get to go to London with Lady Elizabeth, well, I'll be sorry but it won't be the end of the world, after all."

"That's a sensible lass," Mrs. Girdle approved, opening a door off a narrow landing. "Here you are, then. His Grace sent up a tray of provisions for you, over there on the little table. Bread and cheese, he ordered, but I told Cook to put in a few lemon jumbles."

Martha smiled at her. "Thank you, ma'am."

"You have all the needles and pins and thread and such you need, do you?"

"Oh yes," Martha said with confidence, "not like some places I sew where they measure every inch of thread you use!"

"I should hope not, in the duke's household! I had the fire made up, and there's plenty of coals and candles. I'll leave you then, my dear. Lady Elizabeth will come up presently to tell you what she wants."

Martha bobbed a curtsy, and the housekeeper left.

The big octagonal room was Martha's favourite place to work. Its mullioned windows overlooked all the countryside about. Beyond the gardens stretched the green turf of the park, cropped by cattle, sheep, and fallow deer. Then came farmland, the dark brown of ploughed fields chequered with the green of winter wheat. A twisting ribbon of pollarded willows showed where the stream meandered across the flat fields. To the south, the village was a knot of bare, grey-brown trees and pale-gold thatch, with the church tower rising at one end, the mill at the other.

The room was a bit chilly at this time of year, although the sun shone in through the windows on the south side. Martha went to the fireplace to warm her fingers before she took off her cloak. Then she turned to the big table in the centre of the room.

On the table lay a bulky bale, wrapped in brown paper and string. It must contain the luxurious materials she was to make up. She was eager to see them.

She had untied one knot when Lady Elizabeth came in. A tall, pale, plump young lady, she had an unfortunate preference for yellow and green gowns adorned with multiple ruffles and bows. Martha had never quite dared to point out that they made her ladyship look sallow and even plumper.

Lady Elizabeth was followed by a footman liveried in royal blue and white. Albert was a younger son of Farmer Winslow, over at Grey Dike Farm. Martha had known him all her life. He gave her a quick wink as he set on the table a pile of new issues of *La Belle Assemblée, Ackermann's Repository of the Arts,* and the *Ladies' Magazine.*

Dismissing him, her ladyship turned to Martha, who curtsied.

"As I expect you know, Martha, Cousin Edward has persuaded my brother I must have a Season in London," said Lady Elizabeth excitedly. "Is it not splendid?"

"Oh yes, my lady!"

"I daresay you will be happy to see the great city, too. Reginald says you may be my abigail if you make my gowns well, and I know you will. I assured him you are an excellent seamstress."

"Thank you, my lady," Martha said with fervour.

"I daresay I shall quite like to have someone from home as my personal maid. Doubtless you will soon learn to dress my hair in the latest mode, for you are quite a clever girl. You can read, can you not?"

"Yes, my lady. Our vicar's wife taught me."

"Excellent. Look here, at these magazines. I have marked the plates of all the dresses I want, and written down notes as to the colours and any changes in design or ornament. Mama is not to have any say in my choice. My brother says her notions are shockingly old-fashioned and provincial."

Her Grace did indeed favour more elaborate dress than was the current mode. Though Martha held her tongue rather than agree with criticism of the duchess, she hoped that without her mother's influence, Lady Elizabeth might opt for more flattering simplicity.

"My brother says you are not to be disturbed at your work until every single gown is ready, so you must take all the measurements you need now."

"Yes, my lady."

Martha helped Lady Elizabeth take off her morning dress of soft, warm merino in a peculiarly sickly shade of yellowish brown. Her ladyship shivered in her shift while Martha busied herself with her measuring tape, writing down figures as tiny and neat as her stitches.

Lady Elizabeth dressed and departed, and Martha returned to the bale on the table. Untying the last knot, she opened the paper to reveal a vast quantity—ells and ells—of plain white muslin.

Puzzled, she glanced around the room, then under the table. Nowhere did she see any parcels that might contain other fabrics. The small cupboard held nothing but the usual needles, pins, scissors, and thread. The old cedar chest against the wall contained as al-

ways scraps of ribbon and lace, odd buttons and
beads, spangles, faded silk flowers, bits and pieces of
cloth that might come in handy some day.

No doubt the duke's footmen would shortly bring
up all she needed. Closing the lid of the chest, she
turned.

In the doorway stood his Grace himself, lounging
against the doorpost and regarding her with a curious smugness. He was as handsome as her brief
glimpse had suggested, tall and dark, his shooting
jacket and buckskins molded to his powerful figure.
His boots gleamed so, Martha could hardly believe
they were made of leather.

With difficulty tearing her gaze from his splendour,
Martha curtsied low.

"Miller claims you can make a ball gown from a
scrap of muslin in the wink of an eye," he drawled.
"M'cousin swears you can't."

"Lord Tarnholm, your Grace?" Martha ventured,
wondering why the baron should speak ill of her.
Though she had never had cause to exchange a word
with him, she had often seen him riding or driving
through the village, and sometimes in this very
house, when she came here to sew. Surely he must
know his aunt and his cousins were satisfied with her
needlework.

"Lord Tarnholm," the duke confirmed. "He vows
your father exaggerates. Well, I'm a reasonable man.
I shall make allowances."

"Thank you, your Grace." Knowing her father,
Martha bit her lip, beginning to worry. What exactly
had Pa promised on her behalf?

"Not at all." The duke waved a gracious hand. "You
can start with the simple stuff. Make up a couple of

dozen morning gowns and walking dresses and such-
like by tomorrow morning and I'll pay you well—by
country standards, that is," he added quickly.

"T-two dozen, your Grace?" she faltered, bewildered. "By tomorrow?"

Twenty-four gowns in twenty-four hours! He might
as well ask her to spin straw into gold. What could
anyone possibly want with twenty-four gowns? Dazzled by his magnificence, she must have misunderstood.

"That's right. We shall soon find out whether Tom
Miller's lied to me. If so, I'll turn him and his brats
out of the mill to beg in the streets."

Horrified, Martha steeled herself to protest, but already the duke was turning away, pulling the heavy
oak door shut behind him.

"Don't worry," he said over his shoulder, "I shan't
let anyone interrupt your work. I even thought to
have your supper brought up in advance. Yes, there
it is." He gestured at the small table on which stood
an earthen jug and a tray covered with a white nap-
kin.

The door thudded to. Martha heard the great iron
key turning in the lock.

Martha's feet carried her unwillingly to the south-
ern window. There, across gardens and park and
fields, beyond the church tower and the thatched
roofs of the village, the mill's sails turned and turned
in a brisk breeze from the North Sea. There Pa, loud-
voiced and jolly, presided over the great round,
rough stones that ground to flour the corn from the
rich arable soil of the Norfolk plain. The biggest mill-
stones in the county, he was wont to boast, and the
finest flour.

What would he do, what would Mam do, and the little ones, without the mill that was their home and their livelihood? Tears rose to Martha's eyes and trickled down her cheeks.

It was up to her. Perhaps if she worked all night she might manage three or four dresses, even half a dozen, if she didn't take her usual pains to make every stitch straight and small. Tapes instead of buttons, single seams for double, even basting in place of proper stitches where it would not show—considering the possibilities, Martha moved towards the table.

His Grace claimed to be a reasonable man. Surely he would be satisfied with three or four completed gowns!

She stopped with a shock. White muslin. How could she have forgotten all she had to work with was plain white muslin? And cheap stuff at that, she realized, fingering it.

Her heart sinking again, she skimmed through the fashion magazines. As she expected, Lady Elizabeth wanted crêpe and sarcenet and lutestring, with lace dripping from the sleeves, silk roses set on, rouleaux of satin, and even seed-pearl embroidery. Even the simplest morning gowns were of fine jaconet, mull, or sprig muslin.

Beside each illustration, her ladyship had written firmly the colour she desired, primrose, lemon or canary yellow, lime, spring or pomona green.

Martha sank down on a stool and wept.

# Chapter Three

"Miss Miller, don't cry," came an urgent voice from the direction of the door. "Pray don't!"

The sight that met Martha's startled stare made her jump to her feet, knocking over the stool. She retreated backwards, her hand to her mouth.

From the keyhole—but the keyhole was far too small!—protruded a red-haired head. Even as she watched, eyes round with astonishment, a neck and then blue-coated shoulders followed Lord Tarnholm's head into the room.

So he really was a changeling!

He wriggled his shoulders and his arms popped free. Changeling or no, he looked most uncomfortable and Martha instinctively started forward to help. *How* she had not the least notion.

"I'm afraid I seem to be stuck," he said apologetically. "I'm only half faerie, you see."

Dismay at his plight conquered her alarm. "Can you go back, my lord?"

"I might as well. I'm no earthly use to you like this." With an expression of intense concentration on his homely face, he began to move backward, then came to a halt. "Dash it, I really am stuck."

"How . . . how did your lordship do it?"

"How did I get this far? I just wished myself through. To tell the truth, I didn't expect it to work even this well," Lord Tarnholm confessed wryly. "My mother tried to teach me faerie magic when I was a child, but something always went wrong so I gave up."

"It's no good giving up now, my lord. You cannot stay there forever. Could you try a different spell for your . . . your lower half?" Blushing, she persisted. "A different sort of magic, or wish, or whatever it is?"

"I could turn half of myself temporarily into smoke, I daresay. The trouble is, I cannot be sure which half would stay solid."

"Oh dear!"

"I suppose I must try it. If I end up back outside the room, I shall just have to make another attempt to persuade Reggie to leave off this addlepated nonsense."

Martha watched with bated breath. She was not at all sure that she wanted Lord Tarnholm, solid or not, locked in the tower room with her, for all he was well thought of in Willow Cross and environs.

Still, she decided, nothing could possibly be worse than it already was.

Slowly the baron drifted away from the door. From the waist down he had become a cloud of purplish mist. Or rather, from the waist up, for being lighter the mist rose towards the ceiling. Stuck in midair now, his lordship dangled head down, arms flailing.

"Don't turn back into . . . into you yet," Martha warned him. "You will land on your head and hurt yourself." Without thinking, she put one hand between his shoulder blades, the other on his chest, and tiptilted him right side up.

He promptly solidified. His feet thumped to the floor and he caught her arm to steady himself as he stumbled. Hot with embarrassment, Martha found herself nose to nose with Lord Tarnholm.

His eyes were silver, and slightly slanted, she noticed as she backed away. And he appeared to be as embarrassed as she felt, his thin cheeks stained with scarlet.

He looked away. "I'm sorry," he said despairingly, limping towards the table, his crooked shoulders obvious now that he was on his feet. "I thought I might be able to help you."

"To help me? With spells?" She clasped her hands tight together. "Will you really?"

"You have already seen what a mull I make of it when I try to do magic."

"I cannot see how you can possibly make things worse." Her woes returned to the forefront of her mind, and her lips trembled. "Please help me. *Please!* I'll give you . . ." But what had she that a rich lord might want? "I'll give you my lucky four-leafed clover."

Fumbling in her pocket, she took out the tiny leather case Will Cobbler had made for her precious talisman, and laid it in his outstretched palm. His hand was long-fingered, strong yet smooth and slender, quite unlike the square, red, callused hands of the village lads.

As she withdrew her own hand, she felt a strange sensation, as if invisible threads as fine as spider's silk connected her fingertips to his. She brushed her fingers on her gown and the feeling went away.

"The ideal gift." Lord Tarnholm's smile made her wonder for a moment why she had thought him plain. He opened the little case and regarded the brown, carefully pressed leaf with due gravity before putting it away in his inside coat pocket. "I shall certainly need luck as well as magic for this business. Let us get to work."

"What do we do, my lord?"

"For a start, I am not here as your lord, and to call me so will inhibit the magic. I have a faerie name,"—his face twisted in sudden misery—"but I do not care for it. You had best call me Edward."

"Yes, my . . . Edward." Martha's curiosity was aroused. What was his faerie name and why did he dislike it so? She didn't know what to make of him, but he was her only hope to save her family.

"What do we do?" she asked again. "How shall we set about it?"

"I haven't much more notion than you do," he admitted. "The one thing I'm quite certain of is that I cannot make something out of nothing. Shall we unroll some of that muslin? Maybe it will give me an idea as to what to do next."

Lord Tarnholm was stronger than he looked, for he lifted the heavy bale with ease. Martha spread several yards of the white material across the table. He contemplated it for half a minute, then shook his head.

"I don't know enough about dressmaking. In fact, I know nothing about dressmaking," he admitted. "I'm afraid you will have to make up a gown to start with, and I shall watch you and try to learn."

So she showed him how to create a paper pattern by combining the design shown in a print in *Acker-*

*mann's* with the measurements she had taken of Lady Elizabeth.

"Remembering to add an allowance for seams and hems," she pointed out.

While she pinned the paper shapes to the cloth and cut them out, he glanced through the magazines.

"All the morning gowns are basically the same shape," he observed. "Long, full sleeves, a high waist just under the . . . er. . . ." He blushed and continued hastily, "A middling high neckline, and fairly full skirts. With luck, we should be able to manage with the one pattern."

"It will not last for twenty-four gowns," she said with regret. "There are too many pinholes, and sooner or later it will tear."

Fixing his gaze on the paper she had just unpinned from one of the cut-out pieces of muslin, he gestured at it. The pinholes disappeared.

Martha clapped her hands.

Lord Tarnholm grinned, then sobered. "That was easy. What next?"

She took two panels of the skirt, pinned them together, and threaded a needle. Putting on her cheap tin thimble, made to fit her finger by a traveling tinker, she began to tack the seam. He watched closely over her shoulder, his breath warm on her cheek.

Suddenly the needle took on a life of its own. It slipped from her fingers. Dipping in and out of the muslin, it raced around the edges of the pieces.

"There!" said his lordship proudly.

Martha giggled. "Very clever, my lord . . . Edward, except that you have sewn up the waist and the hem! Never mind, I can easily unpick them."

"It is more complicated than I realized." Crest-fallen, he handed her the scissors.

She pulled the thread from the waistline, turned to the hem, and burst out laughing. "See, the needle ran out of thread! Way back here. Never mind, I'll finish it off."

"If I was all faerie, the thread would have gone on forever," he grumbled. "In fact, I daresay the needle would have known where to stop and start again."

Despite a few more false starts, Martha quickly tacked the rest of the pieces together with his care-fully directed help. With one of the flatirons she had set to the fire earlier, she pressed the gown, singing a cheerful song as she worked. The ballad of "Lovely Joan" was one of her favourites, the story of a girl who had cheated her would-be seducer.

" 'Then he pulled off his ring of gold,

" 'My pretty little miss, do this behold.

" 'I'd freely give it for your maidenhead.

" 'And her cheeks they blushed like the roses red,' " Martha sang, heedless of her audience.

" 'She's robbed him of his horse and ring,

" 'And left him to rage in the meadows green.' "

Lord Tarnholm laughed. Martha's cheeks burned, more like glowing embers than red roses. All that talk of maidenheads! So amiable and gentle as he was, she had plumb forgot she was singing to a man, and a lord at that. Covered with confusion, she hid her face in her hands.

"Quick, the iron!"

With a gasp she seized it. She stared in dismay at the brown scorch mark, right where Lady Elizabeth would sit upon it if the gown was ever fit to wear.

He touched it and it began to fade.

Was it her imagination or did the shape change to a heart, just before it vanished away? And if it did, was it a-purpose, or was it just his magic going awry again? She had never heard that the baron was a one for chasing the petticoats, like his cousin the duke. Poor fellow, with his looks it could not be often he got a chance to make up to a maid, for all his title and his fortune.

But she had best be wary, she decided. Like a shield before her, she held up the gown by the shoulders.

"Lady Elizabeth ought to try it on now," she said, "but his Grace said there wasn't to be a fitting, so I'll sew it up properly right away. Just as well, really, that my lady don't see it, for white muslin's not what she asked for, nor nowhere near." Her worries returned.

"Now I have some notion what I'm doing, we shall work faster."

Though he was right, a clock struck three somewhere in the house as they finished. Three hours gone, and only one plain white muslin gown to show for it.

"Now what?" she asked hopelessly.

"Let me see if I can double it."

Sweat stood out on his forehead as he concentrated on the dress. The fabric stirred. He paled and his gesturing hands shook with the effort.

"Edward, wait." In her concern for him, she disregarded the awkwardness of using his Christian name. "You said you cannot make something from nothing. Perhaps we should . . . well, sort of *feed* it?"

Gingerly she picked up the gown and laid it out on top of the scraps left from cutting it out.

At once, as though animated by the magical energy he had poured into it, the gown began to grow. Martha clutched Lord Tarnholm's arm. Under their fascinated gaze, the gown's edges crept across the table, absorbing the scraps of fabric. It lengthened and widened till before them lay a gown fit for a giantess.

Martha suppressed a half-hysterical giggle as Lord Tarnholm's shoulders sagged.

"I warned you everything would go wrong," he groaned, his silver eyes chagrined.

His disappointment made Martha ignore her own. "Don't give up," she urged him. "See if you can divide it into two. Taking things apart is always easier than making them."

A moment later she triumphantly held up two gowns.

As the short winter day faded, Lord Tarnholm struggled to develop and refine the trick of doubling in number rather than size. At last he mastered the knack, but it tired him and he had to rest often. Still, even with a break for bread and cheese, jumbles, and cider, by midnight most of the bale was gone and they had four-and-twenty identical white muslin gowns.

"I had better hire out to Mrs. Ballantine's Academy," said Lord Tarnholm with a weary smile, "to make her pupils' uniforms. To think that just a few years ago unadorned white muslin was *de rigueur* for young ladies on every occasion! I hope I can work out how to produce all the colours and materials Lizzie has chosen."

"I'm sure you can." Martha's faith in him was by now unbounded.

While he was busy multiplying the basic gown, she had sorted through the contents of the cupboard and the chest. She had found samples of almost every colour, every fabric Lady Elizabeth wanted. On each unadorned dress as he created it, she had embroidered a small area, or sewn on a few inches of lace, ruffles, ribbons, or flounces.

Now, taking a dress from the heap, she spread it out on the table and consulted the *Ladies' Magazine.* Beside it she set a length of primrose yellow embroidery silk, a fragment of delicate jaconet muslin that happened to be blue, and an illustration of a much beruffled morning gown.

He whistled. "This is going to be complicated."

"Change the fabric first, without worrying about the colour," she suggested.

Picking up the scrap of jaconet muslin, he closed his eyes and rubbed it between his fingers. Then he felt the hem of the gown.

"They are very similar," he said uncertainly.

"So it should be easy."

"That's what you think!" He flashed her a quizzical smile. "I have not your fine discrimination and I'm not at all sure I can tell the difference. Oh well, needs must when the devil drives."

The now familiar expression of fierce concentration on his face, Lord Tarnholm touched the gown with the scrap of fine, blue jaconet. The piece in his hand promptly turned into plain, cheap, white muslin.

Without a word, Martha took it from him and gave him another sample of jaconet, pink this time. He pondered for a moment, closed his eyes, then tried again. The gown did not change visibly, but when she felt it, Martha could tell it was now finer, softer.

She smiled at him. "That's it. You have done it."

"It was a matter of focussing on touch instead of sight, but also of direction. I can't explain any better than that. Now let me try the colour." He studied the strand of primrose yellow embroidery silk, holding it up to the light of a branch of candles.

Outside the windows, a myriad of frosty stars glittered in the black night sky, like incongruous spangles on a mourning gown. Martha shivered at the thought.

At least the penny-pinching duke had not quibbled at Mrs. Girdle's provision of plenty of lamps and candles. Their light was adequate, and they helped to warm the room. The bread and cheese his Grace had supplied would have been enough for her alone, though shared between two it had made a skimpy dinner, even with the biscuits.

Martha was hungry and sleepy, but no longer frightened. She trusted Lord Tarnholm to save both her and her family from disaster.

An odd chap, he was, not a bit high in the instep. Sort of unsure of himself even though he was a nobleman and half faerie. He could not have had it easy, being on the small side, plain as a pickled onion, and lame into the bargain, while his cousin was so tall and handsome and dashing.

He was rubbing his shoulder now as if it hurt, and shifting on his stool to ease his bad leg.

She didn't believe any more that he was a changeling, a faerie child left in the cradle when a human babe was stolen away. All the old stories said changelings were mischievous beings, always causing upsets, and vanishing away before they grew up. No, Edward was half and half, the last Baron Tarnholm his pa, and his mam a water-faerie, a nixie. No wonder her ladyship kept herself to herself.

His mam was a faerie. "Can't Lady Tarnholm cure your leg with a spell?" she blurted out.

Flushing fiery red, he muttered, "My mother has done what she can. There is a powerful magic against her."

Her well-meant question had turned out to be both rude and unkind. Her tiredness and his friendliness had made her forget her place. Wishing she had not spoken, Martha bowed her head.

He touched her hand, pointed at the gown spread out on the table.

"Look!"

From the hem towards the neckline oozed a yellowish hue. It was a warm, pretty shade with a hint of blush pink—peach, in fact—as if the pale primrose had absorbed a touch of colour from his lordship's cheeks.

Not for the world would Martha have mentioned the glaring difference from what Lady Elizabeth had instructed, but Lord Tarnholm saw it for himself.

"It's wrong, isn't it?"

"It's lovely, and it'll suit Lady Elizabeth much better than what she asked for."

"Yes, I believe you are right." He cheered up. "Now for the ruffles."

He studied the short piece of wide, full ruffle Martha had made and pinned onto the skirt to act as a model; then he turned to examine the fashion plate in the magazine. Meanwhile, Martha swiftly

pinned strips of ungathered muslin to the skirt and
bodice to "feed" the five ruffles.

Glancing back and forth from picture to gown,
Lord Tarnholm made his magical gestures. The strips
quivered and bulged, but failed to gather into ruffles.
He frowned with the intensity of his efforts.

Then Martha noticed that the pattern piece of pre-
sewn ruffle had narrowed and flattened.

"Wait, Edward. Just a minute."

She unpinned the strips. Beneath were rows of tiny,
dainty ruffles. Martha began to laugh, and then she
found she could not stop.

His puzzled stare changed to a grin, and then to
alarm. Standing up, he shook her gently.

"Hush, Martha. What is it?"

"It's just . . . ," she gasped, gazing up into anxious,
sympathetic, silver-grey eyes. "It is just that your
magic seems to know what will become Lady Elizabeth much better than she does herself. The trouble
is, if she is not satisfied with what I . . . we have
made. . . . If she complains to his Grace, he will say
I have not. . . ."

A lump in her throat, her eyes filling with tears,
she dropped her head on his chest.

One arm about her shoulders, he awkwardly patted
her back. "You need not worry about Lizzie. I may
not be able to persuade the duke to abandon his folly
once he has a bee in his bonnet, but Lizzie will believe me when I say she has never looked so well.
Come, my dear, dry those tears."

She took the handkerchief he pressed into her
hand. "I'm sorry. I'm tired."

"And worried about your family."

"You know?"

"Yes, Reggie told me of his threat to turn you all out of the mill. That is why I came to help you." He pulled a rueful face. "Come now, I am tired, too, but we have a great deal of work still before us."

The gowns that emerged from their white muslin chrysalises over the next several hours bore scant resemblance to the magazine plates.

However hard he tried, elaborate trimmings failed to materialize, replaced by elegant simplicity. The colour green might as well not have existed for all Lord Tarnholm could do to produce it. He had a struggle with even amber and apricot, the warmer shades of yellow. The rack in the corner filled with pink, from the palest possible to deep rose, and with amethyst, lilac, and lavender-blue.

They were beautiful. Martha gave up fretting and eagerly awaited each new creation as she pressed the previous one with the smoothing iron.

She still could not imagine how anyone could possibly need two dozen gowns. That did not stop her wishing wistfully that she owned more than three, two of which, including the one she had on, were made of practical brown stuff.

"Twenty-three," she counted.

There was no response.

Looking up from ironing a lace edging, she saw that his lordship was fast asleep, his head pillowed on his arms on top of the last gown. A wave of fatigue crashed down on her. That one could wait; she wasn't going to disturb him to get at it.

With leaden arms, she hung up the one she had just finished. When she blew out the candles and glanced at the window, she saw a faint paling of the eastern sky. Dawn was not far off, but the duke surely had not referred to dawn when he spoke of morning. The gentry were late risers.

Martha curled up on the chest and fell asleep.

# Chapter Four

A harsh, grating noise roused Edward.

Bewildered, his bad shoulder aching like the very devil, he stared around the room. What the deuce was he doing up in the tower?

His gaze fell on tousled yellow curls, rosy cheeks, a delectable figure somehow enhanced by its awkward huddle on the chest. Martha Miller. Of course! Memory returning, he smiled tenderly.

What a dear she was! He had often seen her before, and thought her pretty. Though he had never had occasion to speak to her, he had known her reputation as a first-rate seamstress and an honest young woman. How could he have guessed she was also kindhearted, compassionate, merry, intelligent, wellspoken, and with a voice like a song-thrush in springtime. . . .

Screeech . . . click.

A key turning in the lock!

In one swift—though far from smooth—motion, Edward rose from the stool and stumblingly darted to hide behind the opening door. If anyone discovered that he had spent the night here, Martha would be ruined.

His leg throbbing, once again he scanned the

room: a crumpled dress on the table, twenty-three more hanging in the corner, a seamstress's paraphernalia strewn here and there, stubs of candles. Nothing there to give away his presence if he was not seen.

Pale sunbeams shone in through the east window. The sun rose late at this season: mid morning, then. Was Reggie so impatient as to rise before noon?

"Martha?" That was Lizzie's tentative voice. She stepped into the room, caught sight of the rack of dresses, and ran to inspect them. "Martha!"

She was furious now. Crossing to the chest, her back to Edward, she shook the girl roughly.

He moved out from behind the door, then to the side, so that the doorway was at his back, as if he had just stepped through.

"They are all the wrong colours!" Lizzie cried angrily as Martha sat up, rubbing drowsy blue eyes.

"My doing." Edward smiled at his young cousin as she swung round, incensed.

"Cousin Edward! You mean you told Martha to ignore my instructions?"

At least she appeared to believe he had followed her up the spiral stairs, unlikely though it was that she would not have overtaken him on the way.

"I could not bear to see such a pretty young lady impair her looks with ill-advised choices," he said pacifically. "Yellow and green really do not suit you in the slightest, my dear Lizzie."

She pouted. "Then why have you never said anything before?" she asked, her tone disbelieving.

"It hardly signified while you were still in the schoolroom and hidden away in the country," he

pointed out. "A London Season is another matter.
For that, it is imperative to make the best of yourself."

"Yes, but. . . ."

"Try them on, Lizzie," he urged. "I wager you will
like the result."

Lizzie yielded. "Oh very well. You will have to wait
outside, though, Cousin Edward. Hurry up, Martha,
do. I must be gone before my brother wakes up. He
will be cross as crabs if he finds I have disturbed you
when he strictly ordered that you must not be distracted from your work, but I simply could not wait
to see what you have made."

"Where did you get the key?" Edward asked as
Martha stumbled sleepily to the clothes rack.

"From Mrs. Girdle, of course."

The housekeeper, of course! And he had fought
his way through the keyhole, making an utter cake
of himself, having assumed that Reggie had the only
key. As he left the room, Edward surreptitiously pock-
eted the key which Lizzie had left in the lock.

Waiting on the tiny landing, he leant uncomfortably, sore in every joint, against the chilly stone wall.
Though he fixed his gaze on the narrow, unglazed
window, he was blind to the panorama of roofs, turrets, chimneys, and towers, for his mind's eye was
filled with Martha's image.

Weeping, smiling, laughing, singing, intent over
her needle, sleepily yawning, blushing in confusion,
concerned for his discomfort, cheering his success—
it would be all too easy to persuade himself he had
won her regard.

All too easy to fall in love.

Bitterly aware of his disabilities, Edward had always
avoided the company of females other than his fam-

ily. Small wonder, then, that he should find himself attracted to the first pretty girl who welcomed his presence.

He reminded himself sternly that her welcome stemmed from desperation. Even if he had not started out by humiliating himself before her with that caperwitted keyhole business, she could not possibly love a cripple. Her gratitude must satisfy him.

He was glad to have been able to help her, to prevent the eviction of her family. Tom was a good miller, a good husband and father, even though he was the biggest braggart in Norfolk. Only a gullible sapskull like the Duke of Diss would believe his tall tales and expect the impossible of his daughter. Only a selfish coxcomb like the noble Duke of Diss would threaten to beggar her family if she failed.

"Cousin Edward? Come and see."

Returning to the tower room, he watched Lizzie preen before the looking glass on the wall. She turned to him and curtsied low.

She had put on a dress the pale pink of wild roses, a shade produced by Edward's magic quite against his intentions. It suited her, reinforcing what little natural colour she had in her cheeks. The style suited her, too, transforming incipient *embonpoint* into a pleasing plumpness.

Recalling his struggle with the mother-of-pearl buttons circling the skirt between the rows of narrow lace, Edward grinned at Martha. She did not notice, for her eyes were downcast in the submissive stance of a servant.

Such meekness was all wrong for her, he thought, suddenly angry. He hated to see it. Why should so

bright and lively a girl defer to his cousin—insipid,
Mama had called her, not without justice—because
of a mere accident of birth?

"You have worked *magic*, Miss Miller," he said, glad
to see her soft lips quirk in amusement as she bobbed
a deferential curtsy. "I have never seen Lady Elizabeth look so well. You will take the Ton by storm,
Lizzie."

"Do you really think so, Cousin Edward?" Pleased,
she turned back to the looking glass. "I own it is a
charming gown, though rather plain."

"Surely you cannot want an excess of ornament to
distract attention from your face?"

"I suppose not," she said dubiously. "Let me try
another, Martha. That lilac—it is not at all my colour."

To Edward's relief he was exiled to the landing only
four times more before he succeeded at last in con-
vincing Lizzie that her entire new wardrobe became
her to perfection. He was aided by her qualms at the
prospect of being caught there by her brother.

Quickly she changed back into the gown she had
arrived in, only to stand frowning before her reflection, vaguely dissatisfied.

Consulting his watch, Edward looked grave. "Even
Reggie will not stay much longer abed."

"Oh, let us hurry away! I should not care to meet
him upon the stairs. Thank you, Martha," she said
graciously. "I am quite pleased and so I shall tell the
duke."

Edward had no excuse to linger. "I expect the duke
will be with you soon," he said to Martha. "I am sure
he will be delighted with what you have accom-
plished."

"Thank you, my lord," she said demurely, curtsying, eyes still cast down. But as he followed Elizabeth out of the room, he thought he heard a soft, *Thank* you, Edward."

Limping awkwardly down the stairs after his happily chattering cousin, he followed her into the sunny breakfast room, where they found his aunt and the rest of his cousins. The smells of coffee, bacon, ham, and toasted muffins made him realize how hungry he was—and Martha must be. After greeting the duchess and the girls, he directed a footman to take up a tray to Miss Miller.

"Oh, m'lord, I daresn't," the lad quavered. "His Grace gave orders no one's to go up the tower, and he's a'ready dismissed Albert just for rattling the coals in the scuttle when he made up the fire in his Grace's chamber 'smorning."

"Reggie is shockingly unreasonable, Edward," lamented Alicia, Duchess of Diss, a wispy, grey-haired lady. The over-elaborate gowns she favoured in an apparent attempt to lend herself substance only succeeded in making her look still more fragile and ineffective. She had as little colour sense as her eldest daughter. The puce she wore this morning needed an imposing figure to carry it off in style.

"Albert did nothing so very bad," she continued. "He is an excellent footman and certainly did not disturb Reggie on purpose. And I'm sure the poor girl ought to have something to eat, but it is as useless to argue with Reginald as it was with his father."

"I know, Aunt Alicia." With a sigh, Edward once more addressed the footman. "John, you may inform Albert that his position will await him when his Grace

returns to London. Now make up a tray, if you please.
I shall take it up to the tower myself.''

The footman was eager to make amends. "I'll get
Cook to pack up a basket o' goodies, m'lord," he
offered. " 'Twill be easier for your lordship to
carry."

John even ventured to carry the basket as far as
the base of the tower stair. There Edward took it
and wearily limped back up the stone spiral—fortu-
nately, as it turned out, for he had forgotten to lock
the door.

He found Martha asleep again, curled up on the
chest, her blond head pillowed on her hands. She
had tidied the room, pressed the last gown and hung
it with the rest.

Setting down the basket on the table, he stood looking down at her. His heart twisted in his breast. Too
late for caution, he realized. He was in love.


Martha woke when the late morning sun touched
her face. Within her middle was a growling void. She
sat up, stretched and rubbed her eyes, and noticed
the napkin-covered basket on the table.

At once she guessed who had brought it, climbing
the stairs with his poor, hurting leg. Lord Tarnholm
must be the kindest gentleman in the world.

She feasted on cold ham, buttered rusks, and an
apple hoglin. There were two biffins for her to nibble
on, too. Cook, who was Martha's uncle's wife's sister,
must have tucked them in, knowing her liking for
the sugar-glazed dried apples. A corked jug held
home-brewed ale.

Appetite satisfied, she stowed away the remains in
the basket and hid it in the cupboard. She was just

closing the cupboard door when she heard voices on the landing.

The lock screeched, the door swung open, and the duke appeared in all the glory of morning dress. A blue coat of Bath superfine, superbly tailored, topped skintight, dove-coloured pantaloons. Gold tassels swung from his white boot tops, and a gold signet ring adorned one finger. On either side of his starched, pearl-pinned cravat, his shirtpoints rose so high he had no choice but to elevate his haughty chin and look down his aristocratic nose.

Doubtless that explained his use of a quizzing glass, through which one cold, arrogant eye, horribly magnified, appraised Martha.

Stifling a nervous giggle, she curtsied. He strode into the room, followed by Lady Elizabeth and Lord Tarnholm.

"Well?" he demanded.

"Please, your Grace, I have made twenty-four gowns for my lady, like you said." She indicated the rack.

He went over, beckoning his sister to follow, and gave the dresses a cursory inspection.

"Satisfied, Lizzie?"

"Oh yes, Reggie. They are beautiful. Thank you."

"Excellent." Rubbing his hands together, he returned to the table and counted out five gleaming golden guineas, one by one. "Those would have cost me fifty times as much in Town," he told Lord Tarnholm. "If not a hundred times. I shall save a fortune."

Martha curtsied again, with difficulty tearing her gaze from the coins. "Please, your Grace, can I be my lady's abigail when she goes to Town?"

"Yes, yes, make her a dozen evening gowns by this time tomorrow and you shall be her abigail. Fail and I'll see your father clapped up in gaol as a charlatan."

"Reggie!" protested Lord Tarnholm. "At least let Miss Miller rest before . . ."

"A firm hand, coz, that is what's needed with these yokels. Peasants are bone idle without a crack of the whip now and then to keep 'em on their toes. Tell those fellows to bring in the stuff."

Two footmen bore in a bale of cloth wrapped in unbleached calico. The duke and his retinue departed, and the key turned in the lock.

Martha stood by the table, fingering her gold guineas. Gaol! If she failed, would his Grace not only send Pa to gaol but keep her imprisoned here in the tower forever?

She shivered. A grand nobleman like the duke turned the law to his own ends, and woe to those who crossed him. Even the baron could not stop him. It must be wonderful to have so much wealth and power.

But as for Martha and her family, their only hope was that once more Lord Tarnholm would take pity on them.

Sighing, she began to unwrap the bundle of cloth. To her dismay, the entire bale was made up of the coarse calico she had supposed was protecting lengths of silk and satin. Edward had turned plain muslin into fine muslin without great difficulty, once he had worked out how to set about it. She suspected changing cheap cotton stuff into sarcenet, lutestring, velvet, and crepe was not going to be so easy. He was only half faerie, after all.

She turned to the magazines. Lady Elizabeth had

marked all the most elaborately embellished gowns. Martha trusted Lord Tarnholm would once again contrive to persuade his cousin to accept simpler, more becoming trimmings, which would be a great help.

However, each gown consisted of slip and over-dress, doubling the work, and the shapes of bodices and sleeves varied. This time they could not use one paper pattern for all.

Never one to mope when there was work to be done, Martha fetched paper and busied herself with coloured chalk, measuring tape, and scissors. She finished a pattern for the petticoats, but Lord Tarnholm did not come. She finished patterns for two different styles of overdresses, and still Lord Tarnholm did not come.

Lords had more amusing things to do than to help a poor seamstress, she reminded herself forlornly. He had been generous with his time helping her last night. If he had not, her family would have been turned out of doors.

But if he abandoned her now, her father would go to gaol, perhaps die of gaol fever, leaving Mam and the children to starve.

Her vision blurred by tears, Martha started on a pattern for a puff sleeve.

# Chapter Five

A halting step sounded on the landing. Martha looked up, afraid to hope. Iron scraped on iron. The door swung open and she ran to meet Edward, hands outstretched in welcome.

Into her hands he put a heavy basket. "I have made sure we shall not go hungry today. What, tears, Martha? Surely you did not think I would fail you? The duke insisted on my company for a while."

"I have no right to expect your lordship's aid."

"I was well paid, remember. What will you give for my aid this time?" he asked, smiling.

"All I have is five golden guineas, which is nothing to your lordship."

"Give me a lock of your golden hair to plait into a ring for my finger."

Wondering at the note of sadness beneath his joking, she took her scissors and went to the looking glass to cut off a curl. As she gave it to him, she thought she saw a glistening web of tenuous threads, finer than her hair, stretching between her hand and his.

She blinked and it disappeared. Lord Tarnholm put the lock away carefully in the tiny leather case with the four-leafed clover.

"Let us get to work," he said cheerfully.

All afternoon they toiled, all evening, and into the night. As they toiled they talked, of village life and of the great city Martha was going to see with Lady Elizabeth, of books she had read and books he thought she would enjoy.

She told him about reading to old Mrs. Stewart, the vicar's mother, and listening to lessons at Mrs. Ballantine's Academy, about her brothers and sisters and her suitors. He told her about his childish experiments in magic and his dearly loved nixie mother who lived in the lake in the woods on his estate, with otters and frogs for servants.

Hotiron in hand, she sang the ballad of "The Outlandish Knight":

" 'Lie there, lie there, you false-hearted man,

" 'Lie there instead of me,' " she carolled.

" 'Six pretty maidens you have drowned here before,

" 'But the seventh has drowned thee.' "

Lord Tarnholm grinned. "The ladies emerge victorious in all your favourite songs," he commented.

"Indeed," she answered saucily, "for my liking there are altogether too many tales of deceived maidens dying of broken hearts."

By trial and error they worked, laughing together over the freakish results of his frequent blunders. His first attempt at a scalloped hem turned into a skirt split to the high waist into narrow panels like daisy petals. Velvet grew a nap so long it looked like a shaggy dog. A net overdress appeared with a mesh too large to catch any fish smaller than salmon.

"It will do," Lord Tarnholm joked, "since Lizzie is sure to throw back anything smaller than a marquis."

The fine cording of lutestring silk gave him particular difficulty. At first it came out like thick-ribbed corduroy. After several unsuccessful attempts, Martha had the idea of starting from corduroy and thinning the ribs magically, instead of starting with smooth cloth and creating ribs. It worked perfectly.

The next problem was a fringe of vandykes around the hem and bodice. Each pointed ornament was finished with a little bobble of chenille.

"They look like harness bells," Lord Tarnholm remarked, and of course, once he had that notion in his mind, little bells they became.

Martha picked the dress up, shook it, and giggled at the tinkling.

"I think it is a silly decoration anyway," she said. "I am surprised you managed to make it at all."

"Perhaps my talent has a sense of humour," he said with a tired grin. A wave of his hands and the vandykes disappeared, bells and all.

The last twist his roguish talent produced was Martha's fault. Instead of just showing him a picture and an example of a particular kind of sleeve, she told him the style was known as "slashed." Neither of them was surprised when the result was rags and tatters.

In spite of all the obstacles, by dawn twelve glorious gowns hung on the rack. Martha looked at them and sighed, and wished she was going to wear them, to dance at parties where lords were two a penny and every single one was seeking her hand.


"I say, coz, I've a devilish good notion!"

Reggie burst into the chamber where Edward was catching up on missed sleep. The room was always kept prepared for him as he often stayed the night at the house when busy about his cousin's affairs.

He sat up, yawning and forcing his eyes to open. Then he quickly shut them again, dazzled. Was he imagining things, or was the duke's scarlet velvet dressing gown really embroidered with gold Chinese dragons breathing multi-coloured flames? His magic had never yet produced anything quite so outrageously outlandish.

"What?" he asked baldly.

"I wish you would listen to me. I said. . . ."

". . . You have a good notion." Edward mustered the patience always necessary when dealing with Reggie. Nonetheless, his voice came out a trifle waspish. "I did listen, or at least I heard you, even though I was fast asleep at the time. What is this famous notion?"

Reggie had the grace to look slightly abashed. It did not last. His self-satisfaction bubbled over.

"If the chit's done it again—made all those gowns—and she manages the next lot, I'll wed her, damme if I won't. That way I shall be sure of her services for the rest of the brood. Just think of it, five more sisters to go. I'll save thousands!"

"Wed her!" Edward was too stupefied to be aghast. "Wed Martha? You cannot be serious! Have you forgotten she is a miller's daughter?"

"Of course not," said Reggie crossly, with a pout very like Lizzie's. "I wish you will not always be taking me for a knock-in-the-cradle. That's half the beauty of the scheme, you see, her being of humble birth."

Edward did not venture to voice his conviction that his cousin was either jug-bitten or even more fit for

Bedlam than usual. "I don't see at all," he said. "Why is her low origin acceptable to you?"

"Not merely acceptable, it's just what I need. The thing is, I must get an heir, for you're certainly not going to provide one."

"Even if I did have a son, he would not be heir to the dukedom," Edward pointed out. "Our families' connection is through your mother."

"Yes, yes," Reggie said impatiently. "One way or another, what it comes down to is that I shall have to marry, sooner or later."

"You should have no difficulty whatsoever in finding a blue-blooded bride."

"But a nobleman's daughter will expect all sorts of finery and gewgaws! A well-born bride might even want to join me in Town, of all the ghastly thoughts, though Mother never complained when Father left her down here."

The late duke's only interest in his family had been to ensure that his heir grew up as arrogant and selfish as himself. Though he rarely set foot in Norfolk, the duchess had admittedly always seemed contented with her lot. Edward assumed she had realized long since she was better off with her unsatisfactory husband at a distance.

"But Martha—Miss Miller—wishes to see London," Edward protested, recalling the light in her blue eyes when she spoke of going to Town with Lizzie.

"Then she can go on wishing," Reggie snapped. "I'll be damned if I'll parade a miller's daughter before the Ton. Or any female, come to that, but *her* parents ain't likely to rake me over the coals for neglecting her as Lord and Lady This or That would. I daresay the girl will be perfectly happy to stay here sewing and breeding. She'll be a duchess, after all. What more could she ask for?"

Not a word of argument would he hear. Pleased with himself, he went off to complete his toilet, leaving Edward to wonder if he could conceive of anything more painful than to see his own beloved the wife of his cousin.

He tried to consider Reggie's plan from Martha's point of view.

Unlike his aunt, Martha had not been brought up as a diffident, biddable young lady. She had set her heart on going to Town and she had too much spirit to give up easily. On the other hand, naturally she would be overjoyed to become a duchess. She would revel not only in the wealth and comfort, but in the power to assist her family.

Whether she could be happy as a neglected wife was another matter. Perhaps she might be contented enough with children to occupy her. Reggie's children.

Bitter jealousy flooded through Edward. For a moment he failed to distinguish its throes from a different, peculiar sensation in his head. Then he recognized the unmistakable tingling touch of magic.

Once before he had had a similar involuntary experience, a brief vision of another time. His mother had explained that her own immortal people lived in a timeless world incomprehensible to humans, where past, present, and future mingled. His veins half filled with faerie blood, Edward was capable of seeing events that would take place in his own lifetime, or had already happened, or might happen.

Now, slumping back against the pillows, he saw the bedchamber subtly change.

It was evening. Gaslights replaced the candle sconces; the blue brocade curtains changed to green velvet; a florid pink and green paper covered the white walls and a patterned broadloom carpet the polished oak floorboards.

A young man stood before the dressing table, tall, broad-shouldered, golden-haired. He wore a black frock coat with a high, folded collar and loose-fitting black trousers. When he turned his head, Edward saw that his cravat was a small, modest affair. A fringe of reddish beard disfigured his jaw.

Like his hair, his cornflower-blue eyes were Martha's but his expression was pure Reggie.

"I'll be damned if I'll dress up for the yokels, Uncle," he said sulkily. "They should be honoured that I have accepted the invitation. Father never condescended to dine with the neighbours in his life."

"Surely you do not mean to pass up a chance to bedazzle them?"

Edward recognized his own voice, quiet, persuasive, yet with an irony Reggie always failed to perceive. He looked towards the doorway, whence the sound came, but the scene was dissolving, shifting before his eyes. The harsh gaslight faded to grey midwinter daylight; the cabbage roses on the wallpaper merged, then paled to white; the carpet shrank to a rectangle of Turkey rug.

Reggie appeared in the doorway. "Are you coming with me to see what the girl has produced, coz? Oh, you're still not up. I can't wait to see her face when she hears of the honour in store for her." He took himself off.

Haunted by his vision of the duke's heir—so obviously Martha's son—Edward rang for the footman who acted as his valet when he stayed here. Martha depended on him. He could not let her down. He would use his magic to help her win the duke's hand . . .

On one condition.

She greeted him with stars in her eyes. "Edward, did his Grace tell you? He wants to marry me! I can hardly believe it, the most handsome, dashing nobleman in the world, and he has chosen me to be his duchess. Is it not the most wonderful thing imaginable?"

Edward's heart sank. So it was not only the great position she coveted; she actually admired Reggie. Despite the way he had treated her, the meanness and the threats, all she saw was his outward attractions, his good looks, his splendid physique, his fashionable dress.

Nonetheless sorry to bring her back to earth from her air-dreams, he asked bluntly, "What do you have to accomplish to earn such felicity?"

Her nose wrinkled in an enchanting grimace. "He has given us *sackcloth* this time, to make six ball gowns and a formal court dress. I did not realize a ball gown is different from an evening dress, more elaborate still, and a court dress is dreadfully complicated. Two petticoats and a robe with a train! But I know we can do it."

"What will you give me for my help?"

Her face fell. "You know I have nothing worth giving."

"Nothing?" *Your love,* Edward cried in silent agony, but that was impossible. Now was the moment to pre-

sent his condition: "Then give me a promise," he
said slowly, "that when you are Duchess of Diss, you
will let me bring up your firstborn son. Let me guide
his steps, direct his discipline, oversee his education."

"What an odd request," she exclaimed, surprised
and doubtful.

She glanced from the bundle of sackcloth on the
table to the open magazine lying beside it. The illustration showed a court dress: zephyrine trimmed with
lace, over a lace petticoat, over a hooped satin petticoat, all richly decorated with pearls and silver lamé.
It would not do to skimp on the trimmings for Lizzie's
presentation to the Queen, who was a notorious stickler for every observance.

Not that the trimmings made any difference, when
she had nothing but sackcloth to work with.

"Yes, I promise," Martha cried, "for without your
help, I shall never be duchess."

At the instant she pronounced the words, "I promise," Martha became aware of the tenuous strands of
the web between herself and Edward. It had never
disintegrated, she realized, only hidden itself from
her sight. Now, slowly, it stiffened until slender yet
rigid crystalline rods held them at once together and
apart.

Again the eerie manifestation vanished from view.
Invisible and intangible, it did not affect the physical
distance between Martha and Edward. Despite its
elasticity, though, and despite its fragile appearance,
Martha sensed it was as strong, as enduring as a millstone.

Yet a millstone could be fractured by a blow in the
wrong place.

She had no time to wonder about the significance

of that strange lattice, nor to worry about her promise, for the task before them was the most formidable yet.

# Chapter Six

The sacking was near impossible to work with, difficult to pin, fraying when cut, refusing to lie flat when Martha tried to smooth it. As she wielded the hot iron, a mournful song, "The False Bride," rose to her lips.

" 'Oh, when I saw my love out the church go,
" 'With the bridesmen and bridesmaids they made a fine show,
" 'Then I followed after with my heart full of woe,
" 'For I was the man should have had her.' "

She heard Edward humming the plaintive tune as he struggled to change silk thread to silver, with the aid of every silver sixpence and threepenny bit in his pocket.

Hour after hour they worked together. By now they knew each other's methods and abilities; they could guess in advance what Martha needed to prepare to ensure that Edward's magic was not overstretched.

This advantage was offset by such problems as an asymmetrical overdress looped up with a garland of alternating knots of pearls and bouquets of flowers. Though they simplified the ornaments, it was still dreadfully complicated.

Dawn crept through the mullioned windows, and still they laboured.

Martha's arms were heavy, her hands cramping, her fingertips sore. She did not complain. Edward's pale, tight face and cautious movements told her his shoulder and leg hurt, yet he never paused to rest. Courage and kindness—for her sake, for her family's sake, he defied pain as resolutely as he defied the duke's orders.

Recalling his sensitivity when she enquired about his mother's healing powers, she said nothing. Had he not been a man and she a maid, had he not been a lord and she a villager, she'd have offered to rub his shoulder and his leg. Though magic could not ease his suffering, sweet herb unguents might, and hot fomentations, or cold compresses.

Once she was duchess, his superior in rank and his cousin by marriage, she would see that he had the care he needed, she vowed.

"Don't fall asleep now, Martha," he said with an effortful smile. "We are nearly finished. The very last thing I need is a rosebud to copy for this corsage."

"I cannot make a rosebud with sackcloth. Is there a strip of crimson silk?"

"Here." The green scrap Edward passed her changed colour as it changed hands.

Snip, snip, a deft twist, a few stitches, and a rosebud blossomed. "I was not going to sleep, just thinking about what I shall do when I am a duchess."

With a disheartened expression, he said wryly, "I hope you will not be disappointed. Remember, the duke will still be your master, even when you are his wife."

Fixing his gaze on the silk flower, he muttered, gestured. Two rosebuds appeared, then four, eight . . .

"We only need three," Martha protested, and then gasped as a rich, summery fragrance reached her.

The deep red roses heaped on the table were real!

She picked up three or four, avoiding the thorns, and raised them to breathe in their sweetness. Over their velvety heads, her eyes sought Edward's face.

He avoided her gaze. "I'm sorry, I lost control for a moment. I shall get rid of them."

"I wish I could keep just one," she said wistfully.

"A rose in January is bound to arouse Reggie's suspicion. I cannot begin to imagine what he might think."

The flowers in Martha's hands turned to sackcloth. On the table lay three silk rosebuds, pathetically artificial after the real thing.

As Martha gathered them in a posy and sewed them to the shoulder of the last gown, Edward's warnings resounded in her head. The duke would still be her master, even when she was his wife, and the duke's suspicion was to be feared.

She stabbed her needle into the pincushion and turned to Edward. "I dread to think what his Grace will do if I give you his heir to bring up," she said in a quavery voice.

"You promised."

Frightened now, remembering the duke's threats against her family, she pleaded with him. "Do not hold me to my promise. Please, Edward . . . my lord. I shall find another way to reward you for your help, when I am duchess."

His face twisted and he said sadly, "Very well. If you

can find out my faerie name within three days, I shall release you from your promise."

Shoulders slumped, his limp more pronounced than ever, he left her.

Lord Tarnholm did not return at noon with the duke and Lady Elizabeth. They were both delighted with the gowns.

Lady Elizabeth even gave Martha an impulsive hug. "I shall have the best abigail in London," she cried.

"Not her." The duke shook his handsome head.

"What? Why not? I *want* Martha!"

"Don't fuss so, Lizzie," he snapped. "You shall have a perfectly adequate abigail, but not her. Come down to the drawing room and I'll tell you why."

He strode from the room, followed by his sulky sister. At the last moment he glanced back over his shoulder at Martha and said testily, "You had better come too, girl."

It was not what Martha expected of a betrothal, not the joyous, festive occasion the villagers made of those happy events. Obviously the nobility regarded such matters differently.

She was too tired to be disappointed. Concentrating on not stumbling, she followed her future husband and sister-in-law down the winding stairs and along passages. He stopped at a grand double-door, through which came the sound of music. Flinging it open, he marched in.

The music stopped instantly. The duchess jumped up from a sofa by the fire.

"What is the matter, Reggie?" she asked apprehensively. "Why did you want me and the girls to await you here?"

Standing numbly by the door, hands clasped before her, Martha saw Lady Elizabeth's younger sisters gathered around the pianoforte with their governess. They all stared at their brother.

"I have an announcement to make," he proclaimed. "No doubt you will be glad to learn, ma'am, that I mean to take a bride. I am going to marry the miller's chit."

There was a moment of dumbfounded silence. The duchess's mouth actually dropped open. Then she recovered herself and said uncertainly, as though she thought her ears must have deceived her, "Martha Miller, Reggie? You are to wed Martha Miller?"

"That's the one." He turned and gestured at Martha. "You, girl, come here and make your curtsy to your mama-in-law. I'm off to London," he added carelessly. "While I'm gone Martha can finish making Lizzie's wardrobe—pelisses and such. When I come back, we shall discuss the wedding."

He departed without a backward glance.

The duchess sagged back onto the sofa. Her daughters clustered around her, giggling and twittering like a flock of sparrows, and casting sidelong looks at Martha.

She scarcely noticed. After curtsying as ordered, she stood rooted to the ground, unable to summon up the energy to think what she ought to do next. The only thing she actually *wanted* to do was sleep.

The youngest of the young ladies suddenly dashed to the window. "Reggie is leaving already, Mama!" she cried. "He must have ordered his carriage brought round before he told us."

At a gallop, the four black horses pulled the elegant

royal-blue carriage past the window, and Martha's betrothed was gone.

Perhaps she had dreamed the whole thing?

But the duchess patted the place at her side on the sofa. "Martha, my dear, do come and sit down," she said, kind though still flustered. "I must confess, this has come as quite a sh . . . surprise. I assume the duke—Reginald—acquainted you with his intentions long since, but it is quite new to me."

"He told me yesterday, your Grace."

"Told? Oh dear, not asked? How very like Reggie, to be sure. But of course you would have accepted had he troubled to request your hand."

"Oh yes, your Grace," Martha said fervently.

"I suppose there is nothing to be done. Once Reggie has made up his mind, nothing will shake him, and it is excessively uncomfortable to cross him. He grows more and more like his father, I fear."

Martha could think of no polite answer to that, so she held her tongue.

"Well, well, it will take us all some time to grow accustomed to the idea. Perhaps you would like to go home and acquaint your family with your good fortune?"

"Oh yes, please, your Grace."

"Stay a few days, my dear, while we . . . while we settle matters," said the duchess vaguely. "I must decide which rooms you are to have—I daresay Reggie will not wish you to stay at the mill until you are married. Oh dear, I simply cannot think straight!"

"Do not stay away too long, Martha," said Lady Elizabeth. "Remember Reggie told you to make my pelisses and spencers before he returns to take me to London."

"Yes, my lady."

"Oh, dear, this is all most irregular, not to say improper," the duchess sighed. She patted Martha's hand. "Not your fault, my dear. What can Reggie have been thinking of? I must talk to Edward."

Recalling the fateful riddle Lord Tarnholm had set her, Martha ventured to ask the duchess, "if you please, ma'am, has Lord Tarnholm any other name?"

"His Christian names are Edward James Frederick," her Grace said. "However, when you are Reggie's wife, it will be proper for you to call him Tarnholm, or Cousin."

"Those are all the names he has?"

The duchess shuddered. "I cannot think what you mean," she said with uneasy evasiveness. "I daresay his nurse may have called him Ned as a child."

Martha did not dare press her.

No one thought to call out a carriage for the future duchess, nor did it cross her mind to ask for one, so she trudged wearily back across the park to the mill. As she walked, the crisp air revived her mind if not her body, and she tried to recollect the names of all the men and boys she knew.

Most had ordinary names, like Edward, James, Frederick; like Pa, Thomas, and her brothers, Peter, Michael, Harry, and John; like Albert the footman and Will the cobbler. Will's dad was Obadiah; Tad at the inn was Thaddeus; and Mr. Stewart, the vicar, was Swithin, all odd to be sure, but not quite odd enough to be faerie names.

Then Martha recalled a play she had read to old Mrs. Stewart. The faeries in that had been called Cobweb and Mustardseed and Moth. Had William Shakespeare made them up, or did he really know? If

Edward's name was something like that, she would never guess in a hundred years.

Reaching home, she fell into bed. Not rousing even when her sisters joined her, she slept the clock around and half way round again.


When she awoke at last, Martha knew what she must do. One person was bound to know the answer: Edward's mother.

Lady Tarnholm was a nixie, Edward had said, a water sprite who could undoubtedly turn Martha into a frog, a toad, or a newt if she so chose. Yet a faerie given to turning people into frogs was not likely to bring up her son to be kind and gentle and chivalrous.

That day, Martha could not get away from her family. She swore them to secrecy and told them, all but the littlest ones, everything that had happened at the great house, except her promise to Lord Tarnholm. They were incredulous, excited, doubtful.

Mam frowned and said forebodingly, "I don't know as I wants my daughter being a duchess up at the great house. They're not our sorts of folks. You won't know how to go on among 'em, our Martha."

"I'll learn, Mam."

"Then you'll be getting so high and mighty you won't want to speak to the likes o' your family."

"I won't, Mam, I promise."

"How're we to know they'll treat you right? His Grace ain't done too well so far."

"It'll be different once we're wed," Martha said hopefully, though not without a tiny twinge of doubt, quickly suppressed. "Just wait and see."

"O' course it will," roared Pa. He was ecstatic, his

round, red face beaming so wide it was like to split in two. "My girl a duchess! Don't that beat all?"

"Ye're a fool, Thomas Miller," Mam snorted. "Never could see past the end o' your nose."

Pa paid her no mind. "What the fellows'll say when I tell 'em our Martha's to be her Grace! I'm off to the Pig."

"That you're not!" said Mam sharply. "Not but what they'd only think 'twas more o' your braggery, but look where your tongue nearly got us—out on the street if we was lucky, or mebbe in gaol."

Pa sobered. "Oh, ar," he said with a sheepish look.

" 'Tis thanks to Lord Tarnholm we're not left wi'out a roof over our heads, him and our Martha. And you swore to her you'd not tell a soul."

"Eh, then, your mam's right, I did that, our Martha. I just forgot a bit, but your pa don't break his promises. I won't breathe a word till the banns be read."

"Course you won't, Pa." Martha kissed him and Mam, then spent the rest of the day helping with all the chores left undone because of her absence.

As she worked, the question nagged at her brain: What was Lord Tarnholm's faerie name?

And what would the duke do if Lady Tarnholm refused to tell Martha, and she failed to guess, and she had to give up his son and heir to his cousin?

# Chapter Seven

On the third day, early in the morning, Martha set out for Lady Tarnholm's lake.

She knew roughly where to find it, though no one ever went there. It was tucked away in an isolated corner of the Tarnholm Manor park, surrounded by overgrown woods full of brambles and bracken.

Though the sun shone in a cloudless pale-blue sky, frosted leaves crunched underfoot as she made her way beneath the bare birches. She came to the end of the trees. Pushing between green laurels and leafless hazel bushes hung with swelling catkins, she came out on the bank of the lake. Only a bed of withered reeds separated her from the silent, enigmatic waters where dwelt the nixie.

"Lady Tarnholm?" she called uncertainly, feeling foolish. "My lady? Are you there?"

A plop startled her. A growing circle of ripples showed where a fish had jumped or a small water beast had dived. Martha hoped she would not have to follow it into the depths to speak to the baroness.

At the far end of the lake, mallards were scavenging head down in the shallows while a moorhen bobbed along nearby. Watching them, Martha was taken by surprise when a voice quite close to her said, "Oh, it's you, Martha dear."

"M-my lady," she stammered, curtsying as she stared, her fears banished by fascination.

The head emerging from the water looked much too young to be Lord Tarnholm's mother. The nixie's sleek green-gold hair was bound with a fillet of gold set with aquamarines that sparkled in the sun, no more brilliant than her slanted green eyes. Her smooth white shoulders were bare, the extreme décolleté of her watered-silk gown displaying a superb necklace of aquamarines and pearls.

"Oh, dear, I do feel overdressed," she said with a friendly smile. "But why did you call me Lady . . . Oops, I've got in a muddle over time again. Never mind all that nonsense, then, we shall start afresh. Do tell me, pray, what I can do for you, young lady?"

"You *are* Lady Tarnholm?" Martha enquired doubtfully. "Edward's . . . his lordship's mama?"

"I am indeed. You think it odd of me, I daresay, to reside in the lake when there is a perfectly good house. I find it quite comfortable, I assure you, though it is a bit cramped after the Norfolk Broads— that's where I met James, Edward's father. I could go back to the Broads now. The queen confined me to the estate only for James's lifetime. But as you can imagine, I stay on because I prefer to be near Edward."

"Surely not Queen Charlotte? No, of course not. Does your ladyship mean Queen *Titania?*"

"That's what she calls herself," said Lady Tarnholm tartly. "Plain Mab it was till she was elected queen, back around 1550. And to make sure everyone realizes how superior she is now, she gives her courtiers perfectly beastly names like Peasepudding and Beetle."

"Shakespeare had it nearly right! Queen Titania confined you to the estate?" Martha asked, enthralled, her vital errand half forgotten.

"She doesn't approve of marriage between faerie and mortal, dear. Though carrying-on is all right, and she does plenty of it, let me tell you. However, she made a law against proper church weddings. She didn't hear about James and me until too late to stop us, but that made her madder than a hornet, so at my poor dear Edward's christening . . ."

The woodland lake faded before Martha's eyes.

She found herself drifting through French doors, open to a flower-filled garden, into an elegant drawing room. Facing her, Lady Tarnholm reclined on a green brocade chaise longue. She was now demurely clad in blue cloud muslin like the reflection of a summer sky in the surface of her lake, but otherwise she was unchanged.

She winked at Martha.

Behind her, holding her hand, stood a tall, well-built young man, with an attractive, amiable face, his hair tied back in a queue in the fashion of the last century. Martha recognized him as the late James, Baron Tarnholm.

His sister, the Duchess of Diss, young and pretty but with a familiar tentative air, perched on the edge of a chair. On her lap she held a bonny baby swathed in a long lace christening gown and cap. Her husband, but for his powdered hair the very image of his son Reginald, the present duke, stood beside her, looking bored. Two or three older people Martha did not know sat in a group.

Over this gathering presided a youthful Swithin Stewart, Vicar of Willow Cross, in his clerical bands. As Martha watched, he picked up a silver chalice of holy water and took a step towards where the baby lay gurgling placidly in his godmother's arms.

A small, lithe mannikin dressed all in Lincoln green with a red cap darted in through the French doors, crying out, "Daphne, 'ware the queen! 'Ware Mab!"

Lady Tarnholm sprang to her feet and ran towards her child. Halfway there she stopped, rooted to the Wilton carpet, as a swarm of slender sprites rushed into the room in a smoky swirl of gossamer draperies.

Their leader, tall and beautiful, crowned with a garland of rare orchids, laughed a silvery laugh with a spiteful undertone. "Aha, the baby in the duchess's arms. This is a task for you, Peppercorn."

One of her followers moved forward, her grin revealing pointed teeth. She began to recite an incantation, and as she spoke, Martha saw to her horror the baby's little face melting and changing.

" 'I speak severely to my boy,

" 'I beat him when he sneezes;

" 'For he can thoroughly enjoy

" 'The pepper when he . . . ' Aa . . . aaa . . . atchooo."

Lady Tarnholm was vigorously shaking a tiny, lace-edged handkerchief at her, shouting "Off with her head! Off with her head!"

Except for Martha, who was not really there, all the humans in the room started to sneeze helplessly, including the baby. His nose had turned into a pig's snout, his tiny hands into pointed trotters.

"Stickleback!" shouted the queen.

Peppercorn retreated, still sneezing, but the rest of the faerie court were unaffected by Lady Tarnholm's counter-spell. Another came forward, hands slowly waving like a fish's fins. The baby's eyes grew fishy, and silvery scales covered his piggy ears.

Perhaps Queen Mab had forgotten that her rebellious subject was a water sprite. Lady Tarnholm had considerable power over aquatic creatures, and as she fought back with words and gestures, her son's features distorted again, changing back towards humanity.

"Toadstool!" Mab shrieked.

Again a water creature: In the battle, the baby's skin shifted between pink and muddy greenish-brown, warts erupted and vanished, eyes protruded and subsided. But Toadstool had no real connection with toads. Lady Tarnholm was winning.

"Foxglove!" The queen's last follower.

As rust-red fur sprouted on the baby's head, the Reverend Stewart made a heroic effort to overcome his sneezes. Gabbling the words of the baptismal service, he sloshed the contents of the chalice over the infant and marked a cross on his forehead. The faeries fell silent.

Though Edward James Frederick was undeniably human, he was no longer a bonny babe, but quite the plainest child Martha had ever seen. Tears rose to her eyes as she realized that the dreadful contortions his poor little body had suffered had marked him for life.

Lord Tarnholm caught his wife as she slumped.

Queen Mab laughed again, mocking. "Edward James Frederick? He needs a faerie name, too," she observed.

"Stumblebumpkin," suggested Stickleback sycophantically.

"Fumblepipkin," cried Foxglove.

"Tumblewiltshin," croaked Toadstool.

"Piglet." Peppercorn blew her nose on a cobweb and cast a malevolent glance at Lady Tarnholm.

"He shall be Rumplestiltskin," the queen decreed. "I wish you joy of him, Daphne dear."

As she led her followers out, the drawing room faded. Martha found herself again on the bank of the lake.

"And I have had joy of him," said Lady Tarnholm sadly, "along with the pain. Robin Goodfellow warned me just in time to prevent the worst. Edward was the sweetest child, always affectionate and considerate, always patient despite his difficulties, and he has not changed as a man. I could not ask for a better son."

Martha nodded agreement, but she said with a puzzled frown, "I have the oddest feeling, ma'am, that I once read a tale about all that has happened in the past week. Only in the story, the duke was a king, and the miller's daughter had to spin straw to gold."

"I daresay, dear," said the nixie. "These stories get badly garbled before anyone writes them down. What Lewis Carroll made of that pig and duchess business! Or is it the other way round? And Shakespeare—you mentioned Shakespeare—put in a bit at the end, where Oberon casts a protective spell:

" 'And the blots of Nature's hand
" 'Shall not in their issue stand;
" 'Never mole, hare-lip, nor scar,
" 'Nor mark prodigious, such as are
" 'Despised in nativity,

" 'Shall upon their children be.'

"Only, of course, he was too late for Edward. Oberon was, that is. Or perhaps Shakespeare?"

"But Shakespeare was hundreds of years ago! And how could I have read the story of the miller's daughter when it only just happened?"

Lady Tarnholm groaned. "Don't ask. Time has me going round in circles. Why, when you arrived to-day—was it today?—I quite thought you had already . . . But I mustn't say," she added hastily. "It's against all the rules. You will come and visit me again, won't you?"

"Oh yes, my lady, if I may. Thank you so very much for your help."

"Not at all, my dear. I am sure everything will turn out for the best." Lady Tarnholm waved graciously, then performed a complicated twist and, with a shocking display of legs, she dived into the depths of the lake.

Martha made her way back through the bushes. In the birch wood she found a rabbit path leading in the direction of the baron's house. His mama had given her the answer to his riddle. Now she was free to marry the duke without dreading his anger over her promise.

Lord Tarnholm's manor was not at all like a palace, more like a larger version of the Stewarts' comfortable vicarage, a solid, friendly-looking house of warm red brick. Martha walked around to the servants' entrance, dreaming of the day when, as Duchess of Diss, she would roll up to the front door in her own comfortable carriage with the ducal crest on the door.

The housekeeper, Mrs. Wellcome, was Pa's sister's

husband's cousin. "It's nice to see you, Martha," she said. "I don't get down to the village often these days, mostly just christenings and funerals and weddings. You'll be marrying young Tad one of these days, I daresay?"

"That'd be telling, Mrs. Wellcome. Can I see his lordship?"

"Brought a message from your father? I hope it's nothing urgent, for his lordship's not well in himself, if you know what I mean."

"He is ill?" Martha asked, alarmed.

"Not exactly ill, no more than usual with his poor leg and his aches and pains, poor dear gentleman. No, he was up at the great house for three days," Mrs. Wellcome explained, "and since he came home he's been that blue-devilled. We're all worried about him. Not but what he'll see you, anyway, for he don't ever turn anyone away."

Dismayed, Martha followed the housekeeper. Why was Lord Tarnholm unhappy? Was it so important to him to bring up his cousin's son and heir—her son? Did he regret leaving her a way out? She hated to disappoint him, but she was frightened of the duke.

She seemed to hear her own voice echoing in her ears, singing:

" 'She's robbed him of his horse and ring,

" 'And left him to rage in the meadows green.' "

And Edward's voice: "The ladies emerge victorious in all your favourite songs."

But songs were not real life, alas. In real life, a poor girl did not refuse a rich duke's hand for the sake of her true love. In real life, she married him, Martha thought muddledly, as the miller's daughter in the story had married the cruel king who threatened to cut off her head if she failed to. . . .

Mrs. Wellcome opened a door and Martha recognized the room where Edward had been christened. The brocade chairs and sofas were covered with blue-striped satin now, and a fine fire blazed in the fireplace opposite the french windows.

"It's Martha Miller, my lord, wants a word with your lordship. Go on in," Mrs. Wellcome urged as Martha hesitated on the threshold. "His lordship won't bite."

Edward rose from a chair by the fire and limped towards her, smiling wryly. "Three days," he said. "I take it you have discovered my name?"

"Yes, my lord."

Gazing into his silvery eyes, she saw unhappiness, yearning, and an unselfish kindness that was glad for her sake that she had won.

Something glimmered between them, a faint, insubstantial pattern, connecting them with a tracery as strong as steel—and as brittle as glass. Martha realized she could shatter it with a single word.

She recalled Edward's loathing for his grotesque, taunting faerie name and she knew she could not bring herself to pronounce it.She could not bear to hurt him because . . . because. . . .

How could she have been so blind?

"Your name is Edward James Frederick," she cried. "I don't want to marry the duke, after all, because I love *you.*"

And she ran into his arms, and he clasped her to his heart.

# The Little
# Match-Seller

# Chapter One

Once, in St. James's Street, there lived a gentleman by name of Sir Horace Courridge. This in itself was not unusual. Numerous gentlemen resided in St. James's Street, in the clubs and in the rooming houses. But Sir Horace also kept a shop. A tobacco shop. Not that the gentleman had planned to spend his middle and late years as a tobacconist . . . in fact, the shop with its neat sign, "Sir Horace Courridge, Tobacconist," had been established quite without his knowledge while he was Colonel Sir Horace Courridge, fighting the French in the Peninsular campaign.

He might have learned of the shop's existence when he returned, wounded in a skirmish shortly before Napoleon's surrender, but Sir Horace, a man of easygoing disposition and a rather shallow nature, had been absent from home and family life for the better part of five years. It did not occur to him to question why his dutiful wife and elder daughter spent a good deal of time in London while he was nursing a stiff leg at Courridge Manor near Wrotham in Kent. In less than a year, just as Sir Horace was beginning to feel restive, Napoleon escaped from Elba, and Sir Horace promptly followed the call to arms again.

After Waterloo, he returned a hero with his game leg and an additional war trophy, a shattered elbow joint. Alas, he was a bankrupt hero and found his family packing their trunks. Courridge Manor and the surrounding estate were his no longer.

It appeared that over the years, while he was abroad and lived comfortably off his colonel's pay, the estate had fallen into disrepair and barely supported his wife and two daughters. No one had wanted to trouble him with problems he could not solve in distant Portugal or Spain. Instead, Lady Courridge, inspired by the boxes of cigars her husband was shipping home for his future enjoyment, had leased the aforementioned facilities in St. James's Street and supplemented the family's dwindling income with proceeds from the tobacco shop.

At the time Sir Horace was recuperating from his leg wound, the elder Courridge daughter, Elinor, had turned fifteen and began to assist her mother in the St. James's Street shop. They planned to tell Sir Horace, but somehow, the opportunity never seemed just right. Sir Horace was always surrounded by old country friends and hunting companions, by fellow officers on half pay enjoying prolonged visits at the manor. Thus, Lady Courridge left him in happy ignorance until he returned from the Battle of Waterloo, when she had no choice but to explain their exodus from Courridge Manor.

Sir Horace, it must be said, did not blame his wife for the loss of the estate. Quite properly, he shouldered the blame himself. After all, it was he who had empowered the steward to do as he pleased.

And the steward had pleased, when victory in Belgium was proclaimed, to mortgage the property to the hilt and make off with the money.

Thus, Sir Horace, his wife and two daughters, and Lady Courridge's maid, Berthe, removed to a small apartment above the tobacco shop in St. James's Street. For several years, they lived quite comfortably and happily. Daughter Elinor turned out to be a neat little artist and painted snuffboxes to sell in the shop. Melanie, the younger daughter, grew so beautiful that the gentlemen patronizing the neighboring clubs stumbled over each other in their eagerness to enter the shop.

Business could not have been better—until Melanie fell in love, married a dashing young cavalry officer, and sailed with him to India. She visited home briefly, a year later, to beg Sir Horace and Lady Courridge to raise her infant daughter, who did not thrive in the Indian clime, then rejoined her husband in Calcutta. Melanie's removal from the St. James's Street shop considerably thinned the stream of gentlemen jingling the doorbell and lightened the weight of the cash box beneath the counter.

When Angel, Melanie's golden-haired little girl, was four years old, Lady Courridge was diagnosed with consumption. A Swiss hospital was recommended. Sir Horace approached his banker for travel and hospital funds. He was refused, but a money lender proved accommodating.

Leaving Elinor, now five-and-twenty, in charge of Angel and the tobacco shop, with Berthe as chaperone and housekeeper, Sir Horace and Lady Courridge departed for Switzerland. Fourteen months later, Sir Horace returned. A widower.

*Several years passed . . .*

As her niece's eyes fluttered shut, Elinor rose from the child's bedside. She lowered her voice to an almost-whisper. "Then the handsome locksmith embraced the pretty, young flower seller and asked her to marry him. She said yes, and they quibbled and quarreled forever after."

Angel giggled, opening her eyes wide—her absent mama's eyes, cornflower blue and irresistible. "It's the prince and the princess, Aunt Nellie. The Princess on the Pea. And they lived happily ever after. And I really am too old for fairy tales."

Elinor tucked the covers around her niece. "Then why won't you go to sleep without pestering me for one?"

"Because *you* need to hear fairy tales. You need to believe in noble knights and handsome princes who will marry you and love you forever."

"Oh, I do? But pray consider, if it came about, I'd be clapped in Newgate prison for polygamy."

"What's polygamy?"

"When I marry the knights and princes all at the same time."

Angel sat up in bed, her gaze reproachful. "You're not taking me seriously. I am eight years old, Aunt Nellie! And I've heard you tell Grandpapa that I am wise beyond my years."

"That, my sweet, was not a compliment."

"But true?"

Elinor smiled. "How misnamed you are. You should have been called Imp. Now, lie down and go to sleep."

Angel obediently snuggled beneath the covers.

"Why won't you believe that some day a knight in shining armor will come and carry you off to his castle?"

"Because all England's knights have perished in the wars."

"Is Papa not a knight in shining armor? At least, in Mama's eyes?"

For a moment Elinor stood silent, quite taken aback. Then she said, "Of course he is, my love. But only consider, even if your papa weren't married to my sister, he would be rather young for me."

"But I did not mean—"

"No if or but. I don't believe in fairy tales, and that's the end of it."

"But you used to. And even when you started to make up your own tales about chimney sweeps and fishwives, and locksmiths and flower sellers, you gave the stories a happy ending. Now, you finish with quibbling and quarreling forever after!"

"If you don't like my tales we need not have them."

Angel once more looked reproachful, but all she said was, "There's the shop bell, Aunt Nellie. You had better go."

"Your grandfather will attend to it."

"Grandpapa left. I heard the hall door shut just when you thought I was falling asleep and you switched from the Princess on the Pea to the poor little flower seller."

"What long ears you have! I did not hear the hall door. But very well, then. I shall say good night. And don't let me catch you sneaking into Berthe's room with a purloined book."

"Good night, Aunt Nellie. I love you."

"I love you, too, Imp."

Elinor kissed her niece, turned down the light, then entered the cramped room they grandly called the study, from which a flight of steep, narrow stairs led to the shop below. As always at night, a lamp was lit on the desk facing the stairwell. A waste of oil, as far as Elinor was concerned, but a necessity as long as the shop was kept open at night.

Squeezing past the desk, Elinor picked up the shawl she had worn earlier while searching the ledgers for some miraculously overlooked sums of profit. The search had been in vain, of course, due to her neatness. A virtue that, in this instance, might be considered a drawback.

With the shawl settled around her shoulders, she descended slowly. It was past eight o'clock, and she did not want to face another customer. She wanted to—and ought to—spend more time with Angel.

Sometime in the past, she had horribly failed the child, for, indeed, the eight-year-old was wise beyond her years. That remark about her father being a knight in her mother's eyes!

And it should have been Elinor who first noticed when Sir Horace began his regular visits to the large top-floor apartment, where Mrs. Sarah Livesey, the latest owner of the building, had taken up residence. But it had been Angel who alerted Elinor.

"I believe Grandpapa is courting Mrs. Livesey," Angel had said, voice solemn but eyes dancing. "He is much livelier than he used to be, don't you think, Aunt Nellie? And he doesn't limp half as much when he climbs the four flights to the top floor as when he comes upstairs from the shop."

And Elinor could only blink, for she had not noticed anything; neither that her father left the first-floor apartment every night, nor that he had changed in any way.

All she had thought of was the money disappearing faster than ever; that twice they had been late again with the payments to Abel Crisp, the flint-eyed moneylender in Fetters Lane. That her father gambled more than ever.

Stopping briefly at the foot of the stairs, Elinor mustered a smile, then stepped through the curtained doorway into the tobacco shop.

"Good evening, sir," she said to the broad back of a dark-haired gentleman examining a collection of snuffboxes beneath one of the new gaslights Sir Horace had installed in the shop. "How may I serve you?"

He turned. Bowed. "Good evening, Miss Courridge. I hope I find you well?"

"Very well, thank you." She countered the stranger's penetrating and, to her mind, impertinent look with a quelling one. "You're interested in snuffboxes, sir? If you don't see anything to your liking, you may wish to commission a design of your choice from my sketchbook."

"You do not recognize me, Miss Courridge?"

Elinor rounded the long counter holding the locked cash box drawer and various pull-out drawers containing paper, blotters, pens, and other stationery items. About five paces away from the gentleman, and such he appeared to be if she could judge by the cut and quality of his black coat and charcoal pantaloons, she stopped. She was quite certain that, had they met previously, she would have remembered those dark eyes and a face so lean and sunburnt it made her think of the Arab prince she had invented in one of her early tales for Angel.

The gentleman said, "The advantage is mine, of course, since you, Miss Courridge, have scarcely changed in ten years."

"Indeed."

His dark brows knitted at the coolness of her tone. "I have offended?"

"Not at all." She could not help a touch of sarcasm. "Plain speaking never offends me."

Generally, that was the truth. But not at this particular moment. His words made her bristle. Ten years ago, Elinor had been considered plain. Now, without vanity, she knew herself to be of pleasing appearance. Maturity had done that, softening the effect of high cheekbones in a narrow face and adding a touch of curvaceousness to her figure.

"Miss Courridge? Do you truly not remember me?"

His voice, as dark as his appearance but warm and smooth, made her look at him again. With her artist's eye this time, stripping him of sunburn, of harsh lines around the mouth, of self-assurance. And she saw a tall, gangly young man, stiff and awkward in his brand-new naval uniform.

Charles James Collingwood. For an instant, her heart beat faster. He had been one of Melanie's ardent admirers. Such a frequent visitor to the shop that, if the door was kept open, Elinor had recognized his footsteps as he approached. Firm, decisive steps . . . until he entered and caught sight of Melanie.

"Forgive me. I do remember. You have left the Navy, Mr. Collingwood?"

He indicated the black gloves in his left hand. "At my father's death."

The somber appearance of his attire could be attributed to mourning then, not to preference, as she had assumed. "Please accept my condolences."

"Thank you, Miss Courridge. And I was sorry to learn of your mother's death."

An awkward pause followed. Elinor speculated that Charles Collingwood must have come in search of Melanie. Did he expect she'd be unmarried? Like the older sister?

Once more, Elinor felt ruffled. First, he told her she hadn't changed since her scrawny younger days. Then, he kept addressing her as Miss Courridge, with an assurance that showed he did not at all consider it possible that she could have married during these past ten years.

"It is strange," he said, "but I scarcely recognized your sister when I first saw her again. And that was only four, perhaps five years after—"

"You saw Melanie?" Elinor interjected, astonished. She joined him at the display case. "In Calcutta?"

"Why, yes. Once we were assigned the India-China route, we frequently put into port at Calcutta. And, naturally, I saw your sister and her husband."

"Naturally," she echoed faintly as she strove to adjust her thoughts.

A twinkle lit his eyes, but so fleetingly that she would have missed it if she hadn't been staring at him.

He said, "Overseas, everyone is so starved for the sight of a new face, the sound of a fresh voice, that even a minor naval officer is warmly welcome—be it

at Government House and Belvedere House, or at a
private residence."

"Then, you did not come here to see Melanie."
Absently, Elinor realigned the snuffboxes.

And, most likely, he did not merely assume that the
older sister was still Miss Courridge. Melanie would
have told him.

"I came to pay my respects to you and your father.
And to your niece. She's called Angel, I believe?"

"Most inappropriately so," said Elinor, quite distracted by the fact that within a few short moments
she had allowed herself to jump to several incorrect
conclusions. This had to be another sign of the tetchi-
ness that began to plague her shortly after her last
birthday. Eleven months ago.

Charles Collingwood bowed. "My apologies, Miss
Courridge. This is obviously not a convenient time
to renew my acquaintance with you and your father.
It was presumptuous of me to think I could simply
drop by the shop—as I used to do."

"Not at all. *I* must apologize." She smiled, the first
genuine smile since she had left Angel. "Please believe that I did not mean to make you feel unwel-
come. It is simply that Papa is not at home. And Angel
is abed."

"In that case, may I call again tomorrow? Perhaps
in the afternoon?"

"Come at four o'clock. Angel will have returned
from school by then."

"I shall be here."

He turned to leave, stopped, then faced her again.
"The sign in your window—it advertises a novel type
of match. Lit without a flint stone?"

"Yes, indeed. The Congreves."

Charles Collingwood raised a brow. "As in Congreve Rockets? I trust, the matches don't explode?"

Elinor hurried to the side counter where, next to a rack of pipes, she had stacked a pyramid of slender boxes, some made of wood, some of tin. She picked up the topmost, a tin box with a lightning bolt painted on the lid.

She opened it. "The inventor, indeed, named the matches after Sir William Congreve. But I assure you, they don't explode like a rocket."

"I shall take your word for it, Miss Courridge."

Elinor scarcely heeded him. Selecting a match, she looked at it, still with the same degree of fascination she had experienced when its performance was first demonstrated to her. "They are a fabulous invention, really. Magic, Angel says."

"And aside from magic, what sets the match alight?"

"Friction, Mr. Collingwood." She tugged a folded piece of glass paper from the box. "You see, the matchstick is coated with sulphur and tipped with a mix of sulphide of antimony, chlorate of potash, and gum. And all you do to light it—"

A deep chuckle from Charles Collingwood made her drop the match.

"What did I say?" She frowned. "I was sure I had the chemicals memorized correctly."

"I wouldn't know, Miss Courridge. I intended no rudeness, but it occurred to me I should have mentioned matches at the start to spark enthusiasm at my unexpected visit."

He bent, pried the matchstick from a crack between the floorboards, and handed it to her. "You dropped this."

"I was unprepared for amusement at my scientific demonstration."

"I beg your pardon. Am I still welcome tomorrow?"

She met his gaze, now searching and intent.

As if he set great store by her reply.

"Yes, Mr. Collingwood. Of course you are welcome."

It was shortly after ten o'clock when Elinor sat down at her dressing table to brush her hair. Only two candles lighted the chamber, but the soft glow was all she needed—or wanted.

She was tired, and in a month she'd be thirty years old. Thirty years! It seemed as if the step from nine-and-twenty to thirty was not a single year but a full decade. It was a nonsensical notion; she was well aware of it. But there it was, deeply rooted in her mind. And lighting every lamp or candle would serve no purpose other than to exacerbate the feeling of gloom.

Her chamber door opened after the most perfunctory of knocks. "In the dark again! Miss Elinor, you'll ruin your eyes."

In the dressing mirror, Elinor watched the familiar round shape of the housekeeper materialize in the dimness of the bedroom.

"At least tonight you closed the shop before eleven." Pushing aside a jar of cucumber lotion, Berthe set a tray in front of Elinor. "Now, drink your milk while it's warm."

"How many years have you told me that, Berthe?"

"Forever, I daresay." The older woman knitted bushy gray brows. "What's amiss, lovey?"

"I don't want milk. I want a glass of sherry."

"Now, Miss Elinor—" Berthe broke off. Cocking her head, she measured her mistress with a long, searching look. "No sale again this evening?"

"On the contrary." As she spoke, Charles Collingwood's deep chuckle echoed in Elinor's ear. "I sold a box of matches."

Berthe did not hesitate to produce a disdainful scoff. "If I've said it once, I've said it a hundred times. Close the shop at eight o'clock and save the gas for those newfangled lights. That'll earn you more than the shilling from a box of matches."

"Quite likely, since the shilling is not pure profit. But you know Papa won't hear of closing early. The gentlemen on their way to the clubs—"

"Haven't stopped in years."

Elinor stared at the cup of steaming milk on her dressing table. "No, not very many. Not since Melanie left."

Again, Berthe gave her a searching look. Abruptly, she picked up the tray, turned, and marched from the room.

Elinor continued brushing her hair, but it was done without care or attention and probably did more harm than good since the thick, long mass tangled and snagged easily. When she was younger, she had wished she could exchange her heavy, unruly brown hair for Melanie's fine golden-blond curls, which Angel had inherited. But that was when Elinor was younger. Much younger. Now, she was quite content with the heavy chignon at her nape.

Or was she? The tiny stab she had felt when she spoke of Melanie . . . Melanie's leaving . . . perhaps she deluded herself when she attributed that stab to sadness because she still missed her sister. Perhaps it was resentment.

Resentment of Melanie's beauty, which had attracted gentlemen and guaranteed a flourishing business. Resentment that Melanie was free of the shop, free of financial strain.

But, surely not! Surely, she was not so small-minded or mean spirited. Yet her reaction to Charles Collingwood, before she knew that he had not come to the shop in search of Melanie, left much to be desired.

And just why *had* he come to the shop? Elinor did not recall him as one of the young men drawn as much by her father's tales of heroic battles as by Melanie's coveted smiles. No, Melanie alone had been the lodestone that drew Collingwood to the shop. And if he arrived to find Melanie surrounded by admirers, he did not go near her but stared at her from afar, generally from a spot near the door where Elinor was painting snuffboxes and miniatures.

She remembered how shy and uncomfortable Collingwood had looked, as if at the slightest provocation he'd dart back into the street. And even though she had been rather diffident herself then and possessed none of Melanie's eloquence in the presence of young personable gentlemen, she always went to some lengths to converse with Collingwood and make him feel at ease. And she had—

But that was ten years ago. The Charles Collingwood of two hours ago bore no resemblance to his younger self.

As abruptly as Berthe had left, she reappeared. She carried two glasses of sherry.

"Here you are, lovey. And if I wasn't such an old fool, I would've long ago switched the milk for wine."

Elinor accepted a glass. She motioned to the only comfortable chair in her small chamber, a worn armchair with a matching hassock. "Best put up your feet, Berthe. I sense a lengthy lecture coming my way."

The older woman, who had filled a variety of posts from lady's maid, nurse, to housekeeper and companion, depending on the Courridge family's needs, lowered her not inconsiderable bulk into the chair. She leaned back with a sigh and slowly, one by one, raised her feet onto the hassock. Despite the late hour, she still wore tightly laced boots that cut into her swollen calves.

"For goodness' sake!" Masking her concern with a scowl, Elinor knelt beside Berthe. In no time at all, she had the laces untied and was tugging off the boots. "Why won't you wear slippers?"

Berthe ignored her. "Sit down and listen. I don't have all night."

Knowing better than to argue, Elinor returned to the narrow bench in front of the dressing table. Slowly, she sipped her sherry, savoring the sweet, hard-edged richness.

"When I was your age, said Berthe, "I just started thinking of marriage. In fact, I had as much as chosen the one I wanted to get hitched with."

"You did? You never told me. And here I thought I knew everything about you."

"In truth, I had forgotten, it was that long ago. Before you were born."

"What happened? Why did you change your mind?"

Berthe sampled her sherry, nodded appreciatively, took another sip. "It wasn't me as changed her mind.

He found a farmer's daughter. One that had no brother who'd inherit the land. Anyways, that's not the point I wanted to make."

"I did not think so."

"Don't interrupt, Miss Elinor. You know how easy I turn off the subject."

"Never, when you have your mind set on a scold."

" 'Tis no scold I have in mind. Or if it is, it's directed at meself for not speaking up sooner. Haven't I seen you running yourself ragged, day in, day out? For I don't know how many years? Haven't I watched you grow quiet and serious? Happy only when you're with the child. And her not even your own!"

"Since I am not married," Elinor pointed out mildly, "it is just as well that Angel is not my child."

"But you should have a child. Several children. And you should be married. That's just my point! Miss Elinor, when *I* was thirty—"

"I am not thirty yet, Berthe, dear."

"When *I* was thirty," the older woman reiterated firmly, "I was only just starting to think of marriage. But that's the way it is. Most of us in service cannot afford to think of having a family until we've risen to a good position and put by a tidy nest egg. 'Cause once you're married you're not likely to find another post."

"Dearest Berthe, married or not, you would always have—"

Berthe cut in. "But that's not how it is with a lady. A young lady is raised to think of marriage from the moment she learns to curtsy. And when a lady isn't married by the time she's twenty, let alone thirty—"

Anticipating a protest, the housekeeper drank some sherry. But Elinor said nothing.

Berthe drew a deep, audible breath. "Aye, lovey. By the time a lady is thirty, and still unmarried, she thinks of herself as useless. A dried-up spinster."

Again, Elinor said nothing, only raised her glass in silent salute.

Berthe nodded. "She doesn't paint anymore, excepting to dab a touch of color on a snuffbox or two. And she no longer argues with her father, only works harder 'cause then she proves to herself that she's doing her part in keeping that shark, that Abel Crisp, away. And she's always worrying about what will happen to us all if she fails to make the payments."

Still, Elinor did not speak. She could not had she wanted to. Every point Berthe raised hit her with the full force of truth, knocking the breath out of her.

It was a long time since she had done any serious painting. Sir Thomas Lawrence had consented to give her lessons . . . but there wasn't any money. Instead, she had concentrated on snuffboxes, on the shop.

She was a spinster . . . and had stopped dreaming of a man who would fall in love with her. A knight in shining armor, as Angel would call him. The man who would snap his fingers at her shopkeeper's past and carry her off to a beautiful home. That mystical "him" who never appeared.

No, there was nothing Elinor could present in rebuttal of Berthe's claims.

Laboriously, Berthe rose. She picked up her boots, drained her glass, then hobbled to Elinor's side. "Shouldn't have taken my shoes off. It hurts worse when you expose a pain. Drink up and think on that, deary."

Elinor handed over her glass, only half empty.
There was an arrested look on her face.

She said, "It may hurt more, indeed. But, pain or
anything else, when it is exposed, can be dealt with
more competently than when it is hidden."

"Aye, Miss Elinor. As long as you're not talking
about me feet and ankles."

No, Berthe's hurting feet were not what Elinor was
thinking about. It was the exposition of her needs.

And how to deal with them.

Warmly, she embraced her old friend. "Get some
sleep, Berthe, dear. You know Angel will be up with
the birds and wanting the porridge only you know
how to cook without lumps."

"And you, Miss Elinor, whatever you do, see to it
that you show a spark of life. 'Tis what a lady needs
to snag a husband."

"*Snag?* Berthe! What a horrid thought. And how
flattering to me."

"Don't play word games with me, Miss Elinor. Just
you mind what I said about showing a spark of life."

Berthe shuffled off. Before closing the door, she
said, "Think of them newfangled matches you're so
keen on. What makes them special is, they strike their
own spark."

# Chapter Two

As had happened so frequently these past months, Elinor did not know whether to laugh or to cry. And it wasn't anything specific Berthe had said that triggered the seesaw mood. Deplorably, this brittleness of character was becoming quite habitual.

Elinor resumed her seat at the dressing table. She should complete the chore of brushing and braiding her hair, but, instead, she picked up a box of Congreve matches. Removing the glass paper and one of the matchsticks, she blew out the candle on the dressing table. Now the chamber was steeped in almost-darkness, the candle on the night table by her bed illuminating only that narrow corner of the room.

Swiftly and firmly, Elinor drew the match through the folded glass paper. The match flared, its light clear and bright and warm.

Magic, Angel called it.

Elinor smiled. Magic or science, the simple act of lighting a Congreve never lost its fascination for her.

Distantly, the tall-case clock in the shop struck the eleventh hour of the night. Elinor raised the match high and watched in the mirror as darkness dissipated and she saw the armchair and hassock, where Berthe had sat. Next to the chair, against the wall, appeared the outline of the armoire, one of its doors wide open.

She blinked. For sure, she did not keep the armoire open to collect dust on her few gowns.

Yet the door she saw was definitely open. And through it, she saw into a room with elegant Louis XIV chairs and sofas covered in crimson velvet, a fireplace framed in white marble, an ornate gilded clock on the mantelshelf.

She saw a shadowy figure, a man's broad back clothed in a perfectly tailored black coat, well-muscled legs encased in charcoal pantaloons. He stooped to add a log to the fire, then turned and faced her.

Charles James Collingwood.

He said, "I would have recognized you anywhere, Miss Courridge. Your hair—I've always admired it."

She could only stare.

"I wanted to see it as you wear it now, unbound, tumbling around your shoulders."

"But . . . you admired my sister's golden curls."

"Of course. She was the toast of St. James's. It was considered *de rigueur* to admire Miss Melanie's fair beauty. She is still fair, still beautiful in a matronly way."

"Matronly?" Elinor repeated faintly. How Melanie must hate to be considered matronly.

"While you, Miss Courridge, are fascinating. Always have been."

"Fascinating?" she echoed.

"When I first knew you, you seemed aloof, almost cold. But I watched you, absorbed in painting. And I saw passion." His voice deepened. "It made me want to explore how you'd respond to a man. When he makes love to you."

Her breath caught.

Collingwood stretched out a hand. "Come. I've put your matches to good use and lit a fire. I've always wanted to see firelight dance on your hair."

Mesmerized by that beckoning hand, the deep timbre of his voice, she moved toward him. She could feel the warmth of the fire behind him—

"Ouch!" Elinor blew out the match, dropped it.

She had lit innumerable matches since her father began to stock the Congreves several months ago, but this was the first time that she singed her fingers.

No wonder, though. Anyone who saw an imaginary room behind an armoire and heard Charles Collingwood making love to her—and did not even feel astonishment or outrage—deserved to have her fingers burnt.

For a moment longer, Elinor stood quite still. And, indeed, she was standing now and had no recollection of rising. Nor did she wonder about it, caught in the memory of Collingwood's flattery, the memory of an elegant room with crimson furnishings. The kind of room she had always envisioned in her home—when she was still in the habit of dreaming about having her own home.

But what nonsense. There could be no memory of something that never existed, never happened. She had been staring into the mirror, at the reflection of her old chair and the armoire illuminated by the burning match. To be sure, her chair was covered with faded needlepoint, not crimson velvet—but in her armoire hung a gown of bloodred satin. For once, she must have left the doors open.

Elinor felt her way to the washstand. A handkerchief dipped in the water pitcher soothed the burn on her thumb and forefinger but not the sudden flutter of palpitations when she examined the armoire doors with the aid of her bedside candle. Both doors were firmly shut.

Which was just as it should be, Elinor stoutly assured herself when she went to bed. And that imagined view of a room in the light of a match was nought but the beginning of a new fairy tale for Angel conjured by a restless mind. The man looking like Collingwood . . . well, that was the tentative mental sketch of a new fairy-tale character, for which Charles James Collingwood served as model. After all, he had reminded her of another of her fairy-tale characters invented a year or so past.

How the seductive speech of said fairy-tale character would fit into a story for an eight-year-old, Elinor did not attempt to examine.

"A pleasant morning, my dear." Sir Horace, still as ramrod straight as in his soldiering days but rather more corpulent, joined his daughter in the shop. He nodded amicably to the only customer, a stoop-shouldered elderly gentleman leaning on a silver-topped ebony cane. "Lord Woolwich. What did you think of the cigars recommended?"

"Middling to fair, Courridge. The snuff, however, your daughter blended for me last week is exquisite." The Earl of Woolwich bowed in Elinor's direction. "My compliments, Miss Courridge. Did I detect a touch of cinnamon?"

She frowned. "Was it too much?"

"Not at all, my dear. Most subtle. It was the snuffbox you selected for the new blend that gave me a hint."

"Painted with the precious gems of Ceylon." Elinor smiled. "I doubt anyone else would connect cinnamon with rubies and sapphires, or with the cat's eye. You know me well, Lord Woolwich."

"If I were forty years younger, my dear—nay, what am I saying? Twenty years less would embolden me to seek to know you even better. But there's my grandson, Miss Courridge. If only I could persuade you to meet him."

"You already acquainted me with Lord Haversham."

The earl waved a dismissive hand. "A chance encounter in the park. You scarcely exchanged a word."

"Words enough to show that we don't have a thought in common."

"He's a pompous fool, I admit. And a rake. But he's my heir, Miss Courridge, and he needs a lady of your sterling qualities to take him in hand."

"I thank you for the vote of confidence, Lord Woolwich. If, however, I have a mind to take anyone in hand, it will be an impish niece, not a rakish suitor."

"I say, Elinor!" Sir Horace limped closer. "That's no way to speak of young Haversham. Has he proposed? Did you refuse him out of hand? Upon my word! 'Tis the first I hear of the affair."

"No, Papa. Lord Haversham did not propose."

"He would, Miss Courridge." The Earl of Woolwich tapped his cane for emphasis. "You need only tell me that you will accept his suit, and he shall present himself within the hour."

Meeting the old gentleman's quizzing gaze, Elinor shook her head. With a smile, she handed him a box of matches.

"Your purchase, sir. And pray remember what I

promised when I persuaded you to try them. That I shall take them back if they do not meet your expectations."

"Alas! 'Tis not a promise I could make to you about my grandson." Lord Woolwich tipped his hat. "Miss Courridge. Sir Horace. A good day to you both."

Elinor opened the door for the earl and stood outside, watching him cross the street to Brooks's Club and enjoying the cool, gusting September wind against her face. Lord Woolwich meant well. Indeed, it was an honor to be considered suitable for the heir to an old and venerable title. Alas for honor, though, once Haversham took over.

The fop had stared at her that day in the park, raising a quizzing glass to his eye and measuring her from head to toe as if mentally disrobing her. She had seen the obnoxious leer and only with difficulty refrained from slapping him.

And in contrast, Charles Collingwood's admiration last night when he wanted to see the firelight dance on her hair—

Elinor pulled herself up short. That scene had been a figment of her imagination. And she had better remember it and put such nonsense firmly from her mind.

"Nell!" called her father.

She stepped inside. The shop bell jingled softly as she shut the door and faced her father, who always called her Nell when he had lost at the gaming table. Or when he was about to propose a scheme he knew would meet with opposition.

"Did I hear aright?" Sir Horace rubbed his left elbow joint, which was all but useless since his injury at Waterloo and often caused him pain. "Did you tell

Woolwich you would decline an offer of marriage from his grandson?"

"No, Papa, you did not hear aright if you're asking whether I actually spoke the—"

"No games, Elinor! 'Tis what you gave him to understand, and no doubt about it. Don't you *wish* to be married?"

"Not to Haversham."

Sir Horace puffed out his cheeks. "At thirty—"

"I am nine-and-twenty, Papa."

"And devilish fine looking for your age," Sir Horace conceded generously. "However, m'dear, you must admit that at this point in time you cannot afford to be choosy. Haversham—"

"Is younger than I."

"Two or three years. What does it matter? He's a great catch. Most eligible."

"He's insipid and obnoxious, compared to—" Again, Elinor pulled herself up short. Taking a feather duster from beneath the counter, she swished it across a collection of meerschaum pipes. "His grandfather calls Haversham a rake. And that, Papa, is a colossal understatement."

"Once you've given him an heir, you needn't have anything more to do with Haversham."

"Ah!" muttered Elinor. "But first we'd have to beget the heir."

Sir Horace sputtered. "Elinor! Such indelicacy."

"Indelicate? I?" Wide-eyed, she gazed at him. "Papa, it was you who introduced the subject."

"Daughter, are you laughing at me?"

"Of course not, Papa. That would be most improper."

Sir Horace stared at Elinor a moment longer, suspecting amusement in those wide gray eyes. But it did not matter, if only she could be made to see reason.

"Think on it, Nell. Woolwich won't live forever. You'll end up with a title and a fortune."

"Married to Haversham, I'd end up in the poorhouse."

"Don't be a goose. Woolwich likes you. And I'd see to it that he provides for you. Perhaps an investment in the Funds. Something Haversham can't touch."

"No, thank you, Papa."

Sir Horace, however, was warming to the theme, his limp negligible as he paced. "And, no doubt, Woolwich will tie up the bulk of his fortune in a trust for the children you'll bear. Indeed, 'tis precisely what he'll do. I tell you, Nell, Woolwich is no fool! He'd never leave you and his great-grandchildren at Haversham's mercy."

"Papa, how much money did you lose last night?"

Sir Horace stopped in mid stride. "Eh? How much? What does that have to do with anything? And I didn't lose, I'll have you know. Nothing to speak of, anyway. Nell, why must you harp instead of paying attention to what I say?"

"I am paying attention. You want me to get married. Well, Papa—" The feather duster swiped across a row of tobacco tins. "So do I."

"Splendid!" Sir Horace bestowed a look of pride and approbation on his daughter. "Knew you'd see the sense of it. I'll call on Woolwich this afternoon."

"I didn't say I'd marry Haversham."

"No? But, then . . . I don't understand. You just said—" Grizzled brows contracted in a sudden frown. "You didn't accept Brigg, did you?"

"No, Papa. Although, I do admit, Mr. Brigg would be a better choice than Lord Haversham."

"A wine merchant!"

"An honorable and respected man. The only man who has made me a sincere offer." Standing on tiptoe, Elinor swept the duster along a high shelf. "And his shop is right next door. Nothing could be more convenient."

Or more dispiriting.

"No, I say!" Sir Horace snatched the feather duster from his daughter's hand. Tossing it beneath the counter, he blustered, "You've lost your wits! Marry a shopkeeper? Your mother would turn over in her grave."

"Indeed, she would not," Elinor said calmly. "It was Mama who set us up as tobacconists. But there's no point to our pulling caps over it since I do not wish to marry Mr. Brigg."

"And so I should hope! You're a Courridge, and don't you forget it."

"I don't, Papa."

Father and daughter measured each other, and it was Sir Horace whose gaze wavered first.

"There you are, then," he said gruffly, giving his coat sleeves a quick tug. He turned and started toward the street door. "And I must be off, my dear. You might tell Berthe not to expect me for luncheon."

"Papa."

Sir Horace did not stop.

"Papa, when I opened the cash box this morning, I did not see the eighty pounds for Mr. Crisp."

The bell jangled harshly as Sir Horace flung open

the door. He did not look at Elinor. "I borrowed it. But don't you fret. I'll put it back tonight."

Elinor closed her eyes and drew a deep breath. When she opened her eyes again, her father was gone. The irregular tap of boots striking cobblestone told her he was walking south. Toward Pall Mall. Toward the United Service Club, where play was as deep as the most hardened gamester could wish.

She shivered, and the sudden feeling of coldness was not caused by autumn air streaming through the open door.

Or by the appearance of a tall, somberly attired gentleman whom she had not expected to see until much later. And not when she was alone.

"Mr. Collingwood!"

"I'm early, I know." His tone was rueful. "Six hours. And I wouldn't blame you if you showed me the door."

"I shan't do that. But perhaps you won't mind shutting it?"

"Not at all."

As he complied, Elinor had a most advantageous view of his back, wide shoulders, narrow waist, shown off by the excellent cut of his coat. The shape and tilt of his head . . . just as she had seen it, before he faced her in the imaginary room, in the glow of a Congreve match.

He approached the counter, and she said with almost perfect composure, "I am sorry to have to tell you that you missed my father by minutes. In fact—" She gave him a questioning look. "You may have seen him leave?"

"I did. But Sir Horace seemed in a hurry, and there was no point detaining him when we can renew our

acquaintance at leisure later on." Charles Collingwood smiled. "He *will* be in this afternoon?"

Elinor stared at him. Like the chuckle last night,
his smile caught her off guard. It transformed the
lean, harsh face, and yet, the mouth had not
stretched in a wide grin but merely shifted very subtly.
The full force of his smile came from his eyes. Her
fingers itched for pencil or charcoal, even though
she knew she would never be able to reproduce that
look of inner warmth directed outward.

The smile was replaced by concern as he stepped
closer. "Miss Courridge? Are you all right?"

"Indeed, I am." She turned to the shelves behind
her, taking down a jar of snuff and setting it on the
counter for no other purpose than to appear at ease.
"In truth, I don't know when to expect my father
back. I meant to speak to him this morning. Inform
him of your visit. Alas, I must beg your pardon."

"You forgot," Collingwood said dryly.

"I did. But not because we place no value on your
visit. Something occurred. . . ."

She could only give him an apologetic look. An
empty cash box was a very good excuse for forgetfulness, but it was not an excuse that could be offered
a relative stranger.

Collingwood said, "It does not matter, Miss Courridge. If I may be frank? I don't mind at all that
your father is not here. In fact, I hoped to find you
alone."

"You did?" She fetched a second snuff jar off the
shelf. "But why?"

"There is something I should like to discuss with
you. But not here." He stepped around the counter,
took the jar from her and set it beside the other. "I

believe you have a housekeeper. Miss Berthe, is it not? Perhaps she can look after the shop while you accompany me on a walk?"

"After ten years, you even remember Berthe?"

"Your sister mentioned her."

She felt a twinge of fear. "It's not about Melanie, is it? You don't bring news of illness? Some accident?"

"No. Nothing like that. If it were, I would have told you last night. This is a personal matter. A—" He fell silent at the sound of the shop bell.

A footman entered, hung back politely until he was addressed.

Elinor said, "You've come for Lord Ipswich's cigars, have you not?"

The transaction was quickly concluded, and the footman left.

She looked at Collingwood. "You said you wished to discuss something personal?"

"I have a proposition I should like to lay before you. But I'd rather not be interrupted by customers."

"I see. Will you give me a hint what it is about?"

"I would find that difficult without disclosing what should be explained at length."

Searching his face—and now she could no longer think of it as harsh—she suddenly had a notion so outrageous and absurd that she caught her breath. Her mind spun, and she feared that she was goggling in amazement at her own audacity.

She turned quickly, reaching with both hands for another snuff jar. Collingwood forestalled her, transferring two jars from shelf to counter.

"What are you doing?" she exclaimed.

He raised a brow. "Clearing the shelf? Was that not your purpose?"

She frowned at the snuff jars, then at him. "Do you no longer wish to go for a walk?"

"I do. But I am quite willing to give you time to make up your mind whether *you* wish it."

His tone. the look in his eyes, all seemed to hold some significance. But what significance?

As if it mattered! She had no need to worry or wonder. She had made a decision and would not stray from it.

She said, "At this point, no doubt, I should simper and tell you that I don't know what I wish. That it behooves the gentleman, if he is at all interested, to persuade the lady to accompany him."

He looked both aghast and amused. "And will you? Simper, I mean."

"No, I shan't be missish. I'll tell you straight out that I would quite like to hear that proposition of yours. However, I warn you, Mr. Collingwood—"

When she did not continue, he said, "Warn me, Miss Courridge? About what?"

But she had changed her mind, and shook her head. No warning would pass her lips. She would simply do it . . . if his proposition was not what she believed—what she hoped—it would be.

"Shall we go then?" He gave her a quizzical look. "Before you change your mind?"

She felt breathless all of a sudden. Excited, like a young girl in her first season.

And what would she know about that, she scoffed. She, who had never had a season.

Then again, it was just as well she wasn't a green

girl. If she were, she'd never dare what she might have to do.

"I must fetch my pelisse." She was already halfway to the curtained doorway. "And speak to Berthe."

# Chapter Three

They spoke little on the way to Green Park. Elinor was comfortable with the silences . . . as if she and Collingwood were friends of long standing, enveloped in goodwill and ease. And that was strange, considering they had not seen each other in ten years and that, when they did meet in the past, he had been enraptured by Melanie.

A searching look at Collingwood evoked a reassuring nod but no conversation. She was glad; there was much she must consider.

Should she let him have his say first? Or would it be best to forestall him and offer her own proposition? No flower was at hand to be used as an oracle, but there were the posts of a wrought-iron fence they passed.

I speak first . . . I should not . . . I should . . . I should not . . .

What a silly, childish game to play when so much was at stake.

And then they entered the park, all but deserted at this hour. In the distance, Elinor saw two gentlemen on horseback, a phaeton trundling along Constitution Hill, a liveried footman with a pug that didn't seem enamored of exercise, for it sat down every two or three paces until the footman pulled on its leash.

But there was no one close by.

In the Queen's Walk, Collingwood stopped, taking both her hands in his. "Miss Courridge, I must be blunt. I wish to lay before you a proposal of marriage."

Her breath caught. She felt light as air, bubbly, exuberant. She wanted to dance on the grass as she had done a long, almost-faded-from-memory time ago at Courridge Manor, when wonderful things still happened and wishes came true.

Naturally, she did not do so.

But she did give him a wide, pleased smile and an impetuous squeeze of her hand. "And here I worried about who should speak first! You *are* blunt, Mr. Collingwood. And to the point. But you might have said so in the shop, or in our sitting room."

"I have much more to say, and it is imperative that there are no interruptions. Not even from your niece."

"Angel is at Mrs. Grimshaw's Academy for Young Ladies."

"You did mention school last night." He looked contrite. "There was no need then to brave the bluster of an autumn morning. My apologies, Miss Courridge. Do you wish to return home?"

"No, Mr. Collingwood. Let us get on with the business at hand."

"Now, who is blunt? But I am glad of it. And even though I seem to have offended the last time I said that you have not changed, I must say it again. Pray believe me, Miss Courridge, it is meant as a compliment."

"Then I shall accept it as such." And, indeed, it was impossible to do otherwise in the face of his sincerity.

He tightened his grip on her hands. "It is, in fact, reassuring to know that you are just as I remember you. That we can still converse in the same frank manner we enjoyed ten years ago. I haven't forgotten those animated discussions. Your directness. Your vivacity."

"I fear you're confusing me with Melanie. I was quite shy then."

He gave her a puzzled look. "But we used to have such long talks. You were the only young lady I knew who entered into my enthusiasm for traveling the world. For wishing to experience other cultures. You once told me that, had you been born a man, you would pack your sketchbooks and pencils and wander the continents. Have you forgotten?"

"No. But I am surprised that you remember." She tugged her hands free of his clasp. "Shall we walk?"

He offered his arm, but she declined. For the moment, she preferred a distance between them.

"Mr. Collingwood, I am deeply appreciative of your offer. However, I take it there's more to it than the formality of asking for my hand?"

"Yes." For an instant he looked as uncomfortable as the young naval officer she remembered. "I don't know where to start."

"Perhaps it would help if I confessed that I meant to propose marriage myself if you had not done so?"

If he was startled or astonished, he did not show it. Never faltering, he walked easily beside her, but she could not miss the sudden intensity of his gaze, the gleam of something that made her heart leap into her throat.

He said, "I'm honored. Deeply honored. And I will freely admit that your courage is greater than mine."

"You require courage to propose?"

"To explain why I am proposing so precipitously."

Dryly, she said, "You need not fear that I am filled with romantic notions. I neither expect a passionate declaration of love at first sight last night, nor an assurance that you've admired me from afar for ten long years."

"Then you do yourself an injustice, Miss Courridge. I have, indeed, admired you from the day we met."

"Come now, Mr. Collingwood. Let us continue to deal bluntly and honestly. The day we met, you came to the shop with two of your friends who had promised to introduce you to Melanie. You scarcely took note of me."

"The whole time I was there, you were engaged with the Earl of—I don't remember, but he carried a walking stick. Ebony with a silver top. He was very particular about a design for an enameled snuffbox."

"Persnickety," said Elinor, staring at Collingwood. "Lord Woolwich was the gentleman in question, and he was extremely persnickety. I did not know you paid attention."

"You did not know because you never looked my way. You were intent on your work."

But she had stolen a glance at him now and again—to see him watching Melanie flirt with his friends.

Collingwood said, "You were very patient with Lord Woolwich."

"He was a valued customer. Indeed, he still is. And now he trusts my judgment in snuffboxes. And in snuff."

"As I said, or tried to say, you are a lady of admirable qualities. I knew it even as a callow youth. And nothing I learned about you since has made me change my mind."

This startled her. "From whom—lud! Did you discuss me with my sister?"

"Discuss you? No, Miss Courridge, I am not so lost to propriety. But you can hardly blame your sister for extolling your virtues to someone who knew you both."

"My—virtues?" Elinor choked on the word. "Did Melanie put you up to offering for me?"

"Certainly not. She told me what excellent care you take of her little girl. Of your father."

Elinor stopped in her stride. Facing Collingwood, she crossed her arms, sliding her hands into the sleeves of her pelisse. "It's hardly a virtue to look after someone you love. And if you're serious about the proposal of marriage, you need to know that Angel is part of my life. A part of me. I would not leave her with my father."

"I wouldn't ask it of you. Collingwood Court can more than accommodate the three of us." Once more he offered his arm. "Please, Miss Courridge, let us keep moving. I don't wish to be responsible for your catching a chill."

After some slight hesitation, she accepted. "But let us turn and walk toward St. James's Palace. I don't care to view the mountains of rubble created by the Waterworks Company in this corner of the park."

"A different name for rubble is progress, Miss

Courridge." But he turned obligingly. "A reservoir will mean an assured water supply."

Two boys, about ten years of age, darted out of one of the houses backing onto the park. Between them, they carried a large red-and-silver kite. A young man, their tutor mayhap, pursued them energetically until they reached the top of a hillock, where all three went about the serious business of flying the kite.

"I am four-and-thirty," Collingwood mused. "If I am ever to fly a kite with a son or daughter before I require a cane, I must marry soon."

"If setting up your nursery is important to you, should you not be looking for a woman considerably younger than I?"

"A schoolroom miss? And listen to empty chatter day in, day out? No, thank you, Miss Courridge."

His easy dismissal of youth was gratifying to one who had become self conscious about the increased number of years in her dish.

He said, "I made up my mind some time ago to propose to *you*."

"Some time ago?" She turned her head sharply, searching his face. "But why did you never—Mr. Collingwood, this is confusing. Indeed, it is hard to believe when you haven't come near me in ten years."

"I've scarcely been home. Not at all these past three years, or I would most certainly have called on you." He stopped, faced her, once more taking her hands in his. "I have not in all my travels encountered a lady quite like you. I've told you that I admire you greatly. Let me also assure you—"

"Mr. Collingwood, I already said yes. Or, if I did not, I say so now."

"Wait! Before you accept my offer, you must hear why I cannot, as I planned, court you at leisure and as you deserve it."

"If it's the period of mourning you're concerned about, we can marry quietly. In fact, I would not want trumpets and fanfare at my wedding."

"Yes, of course. But there is more. Will you listen without interrupting?"

"Very well. But, in fairness, you shall then listen to my reason for accepting so promptly. Above all, we shall deal truthfully with each other. Do you agree, Mr. Collingwood?"

His face was serious, harsh; his eyes intent on her. "Collingwood Court is deeply encumbered. I shall come about, never fear! I shan't even need a penny from you or your father. But, Miss Courridge, what I do need—immediately—is an announcement to my creditors of our forthcoming marriage."

"No." She felt ill. "It's impossible. I'm afraid you're laboring under a misapprehension."

"I know I must appear a fortune hunter. But I swear I'm not asking for funds. As soon as the creditors know that I am about to wed the daughter of Sir Horace Courridge, most popular tobacconist in town, they will gladly extend—"

"They will hound you, Mr. Collingwood!" She wished she had the willpower to pull her hands from his clasp. But she was trembling and clung tightly in the hope that his steadiness would transfer to her.

She said, " 'Most popular' may have applied when Melanie presided in the shop. But not now. And when my mother was ill, my father borrowed from a moneylender. Later, he borrowed again. There were payments missed, others late. In short, Papa owes more than he can ever repay in his lifetime."

Collingwood's face looked strangely gray beneath the sunburn. "How much?"

"Eleven thousand pounds."

He winced.

In defense of her father, she said, "Almost half of that is accumulated interest. But you can see that marrying me would not help you at all. And if you had any business sense and made inquiries, you would have known that."

"I would, indeed. And did you make inquiries about me, Miss Courridge?"

Elinor freed her hands. She was quite steady now, except for a hollow feeling inside her, an overwhelming sense of disappointment. Forcing herself to step firmly, purposefully, she set out for the park exit. Collingwood strode just as purposefully beside her.

She gave him a sidelong look. "Since I cannot be of help to you, and you cannot help me, it is impossible for us to marry."

"It would be ill-advised, indeed, Miss Courridge. But I shall not withdraw my offer."

"Then I must refuse you."

"We could scrape by."

"It is not a question of 'us' scraping by, Mr. Collingwood. I shall be—" She hesitated, started again. "I shall be thirty years old next month. I want a home of my own. A secure home, not one that may be lost to creditors, as happened with Courridge Manor when I was a child. I want Papa out of the moneylender's clutches. And I want security for Angel and Berthe."

"Laudable objectives. Fair enough reasons to accept a proposal of marriage."

Elinor looked straight ahead. "Only now it cannot be yours."

They continued in silence and, as on the way to the park, it was once more a shared, companionable silence. And yet, she thought, how different was this walk compared to the other. Gone was the excitement, replaced by regret and a sense of loss.

Berthe's exhortations the previous night had made her face the truth: she wanted marriage; a life away from the tobacco shop. The talk with her father forced her to acknowledge that it must be an advantageous marriage. When Collingwood spoke of a proposition, she had made up her mind to marry him.

Just like that, at the proverbial snap of her fingers, had she made up her mind. She had always liked him. In truth, if he hadn't been one of Melanie's admirers, she might have—

But never mind that. What might have been had nothing to do with the matter at hand. The point was, she had not for an instant suspected that he was as impoverished as she.

"I shall be in town awhile longer," said Collingwood. "I would like to see you again."

Torn from her musings, she realized that they had turned into St. James's Street, no longer as quiet as when they started out. Elegantly attired gentlemen were now about their business, to read the papers at a club, to be measured for boots or a new coat.

In the distance, she saw Berthe outside the shop. She was leaning on her broom and talking to Edwin Brigg, the wine merchant from next door. A gentle but persistent suitor, whom Elinor had turned down at least a dozen times.

And might be accepting the next time he offered for her hand.

"Miss Courridge." Collingwood's tone was urgent. "I am determined to see you again."

"There is no point, Mr. Collingwood."

She looked at him and again was aware of regret. Against her better judgment, she added, "But, of course, if you wish to see my father and Angel? Or if you need more matches . . . ?"

"I shall definitely need matches. Tomorrow."

"But you bought a box only yesterday."

"I used a great many last night. And shall probably use quite a few again this evening." A smile lurked in his eyes. "Do you believe in magic, Miss Courridge?"

"Less than I did in my salad days. Why?"

"When I lit the first match last night, I saw you in its flame."

He was still smiling at her, and she felt quite strange. Not because of what he said, which should have startled her, to say the least; but because the warmth of his gaze made her pulse race and her heart beat faster.

"Your hair was down," he said, lowering his voice at the approach of two mincing dandies. "And you looked just as beautiful and enticing as I had always imagined when all of us whippersnappers still mooned around your sister."

Now his words did startle her. So much that she was rendered speechless.

"Don't you agree that some sort of magic must have been at work?" he asked.

"I suppose so." She strove for a light tone. "If you lit the match at the witching hour?"

"The clock had just struck eleven."

Thinking of her own experience, that wild flight of a spinster's imagination at eleven o'clock the previous night, she could no longer meet his gaze.

"You doubt me, Miss Courridge? But in truth, I had been thinking about you all the way back from the shop. 'Twas no surprise then to see you appear in the light of the match you sold me. And it was only that first match that was magical. Any others I lit showed me nothing but a cold and dismal room."

"Then you had best not waste another shilling." She saw Edwin Brigg looking her way, bow deeply, then turn to his own shop. He had to stoop to ease his tall, gangly body inside. Berthe also disappeared.

"Mr. Collingwood—"

"I know what you're about to say," he interrupted. "That I should be looking for an heiress, a rich widow."

Again, she strove for a light tone. "A moneylender's daughter?"

"Quite. Does the gentleman your father honored with his patronage have a daughter?"

"I don't know. And I doubt he's a gentleman. I wonder, though. . . ."

"What?"

"Whether Abel Crisp is married. He's the man who obliged Papa. If I married him—"

"I hope you're jesting!"

"Of course I am. On the other hand, he can scarcely be worse than Haversham." She smiled ruefully. "A fine pair we are. Pockets to let. Dreaming of an advantageous marriage."

"Who is Haversham?"

"Lord Woolwich's heir."

"A contender for your hand?"

"Mr. Collingwood, are you interrogating me?"

"Yes." Dark brows knitted. "Because I like you and don't want to see you trapped in an intolerable situation."

Something in his gaze made her tremble again. Now *that* was an intolerable situation. Thank goodness they had arrived at the shop.

She extended her hand. "Goodbye, Mr. Collingwood. I have enjoyed the walk."

"I shall see you tomorrow, Miss Courridge." A firm, brief clasp, and he strode off toward Piccadilly.

Elinor had no time to sort out whether she was gratified or piqued by Charles Collingwood's obliging response to her dismissal. Out of the building's main door stepped the owner, the Widow Livesey, resplendent in a pelisse of emerald green wool richly trimmed with ermine. Short white boots of the glossy patent leather that had become all the rage covered plump feet, and a turban of ermine adorned with three peacock feathers crowned a riot of coppery-golden curls.

"Good morning, Miss Courridge." Sarah Livesey's rouged mouth curved merrily; plump pink cheeks dimpled. "And isn't it a delightful one? Just cool enough to take my new outfit for an airing. What d'you say, dearie? Am I too early with these furs and all?"

"I am no expert in fashions, ma'am. But you shouldn't worry. It's your pelisse. Your hat. They obviously give you pleasure. So, simply enjoy them whenever you wish."

The widow beamed. "Now that is spoken like a true lady! Which your are, of course. And I'll try to remember next time I fret over a gown or a nice bit of lace. Was that your beau I saw leaving? A fine pair of legs, if you'll permit me to express an opinion. No padding of the shoulders either, I don't doubt."

"I wouldn't know, Mrs. Livesey. He's not my beau." Regrettably. The thought was quickly banished. "Merely an old acquaintance."

"If you say so, dearie." Mrs. Livesey started to move on, hesitated, then, before Elinor could enter the tobacco shop, addressed her again. "Miss Courridge, I mean no offense, especially with you always treating me so polite and all, like I was a lady. But I've got a business head on my shoulders. Didn't get so plump in the pocket by being mealymouthed about what's due me and mine. So I'm simply going to speak up."

With a sinking feeling, Elinor rejoined her landlady. "The rent, Mrs. Livesey?"

"Aye, dearie. Two months' worth."

Elinor could not speak. Sir Horace had put himself in charge of personally delivering the August and September rents.

Mrs. Livesey's eyes were kind but shrewd. "You know, I daresay, that your papa comes to play cards upstairs. Doesn't have a head for cards, or for business, the dear man. I suppose it was the rent I won from him?"

"If you could wait another month?" Elinor racked her brains for some assurance that next month would be different from this one or the previous. But there was no assurance. "Is it possible to wait? Please?"

Mrs. Livesey deliberated for a moment. "I don't like to wait. Never was very patient. But we could say that I took from Sir Horace what was mine. And we'll call it quits."

"What you took? Do you mean what you won at cards?"

"It's mostly me he plays with, you see. Two-handed whist. Wouldn't let him play with some of my friends in any case. Sharkers they'd be called in some quarters. But no harm done as long as they keep the play to themselves. So what do you say, Miss Courridge? Let your father continue to visit upstairs and have a bit of fun, and I'll consider it rent paid."

"That is very generous, I'm sure. But it won't do."

A gentleman tipped his hat, entered the tobacco shop.

"It's common sense," said Mrs. Livesey, drawing Elinor back a little ways into the relative privacy of the main doorway. "As I told you, dearie, your father has no head for business at all."

"I agree. But you mustn't accept the money he loses to you in lieu of rent."

"Why not?"

"Because—" Elinor was at a loss. There was no way to explain without putting her father in a bad light. Though how much worse could he look, after gambling away the rent?

Resignedly, she merely repeated, "It won't do."

Once more the older woman studied Elinor shrewdly. "Plays at the clubs, too, does he? And loses? Now *that* we can't allow. Why, he might lose so much that he wouldn't have a ha'penny's stake for our little games. Then I truly would be out my rent. So what's to be done, Miss Courridge?"

"I don't—" Elinor broke off, staring at the widow, plump and very pleasing to look at. Angel had wondered if Sir Horace was courting her. Elinor did not know, but it wouldn't be the worst he could do.

On the contrary.

"Mrs. Livesey, why don't you speak to him? Advise him not to gamble away the rent."

Or the payments to Abel Crisp.

"Oh, I couldn't, Miss Courridge!" Pink cheeks turned pinker. "That's why I came to you. I couldn't possibly speak about rents to Sir Horace. He . . . he's a baronet!"

Elinor lowered her gaze. She had already said far too much; she certainly should not compound what clearly was filial disloyalty.

She said, "Ma'am, Sir Horace is a baronet living in the shadow of debtor's prison."

She noted Mrs. Livesey's gasp and warned herself that she was meddling ruthlessly and inexcusably. Even though she spoke nothing but the truth. And then, who'd have thought the lively, needle-witted widow was intimidated by a title?

She said, "Papa has always enjoyed a game of cards, but he did not gamble recklessly. Not until Mama died. It was she who had the head for business. And without a wife to guide him, Papa is quite . . . helpless. So, you see, Mrs. Livesey, if you were to interest yourself in his affairs, we'd all be well served."

And with those words hanging between them, Elinor fled into the shop.

Surely she was the most horrid, most selfish daughter a man could be saddled with.

# Chapter Four

All day long, Elinor alternately berated and reassured herself. She was, indeed, a horrid daughter to meddle in her father's affairs. And worse, to expose his weakness to a pleasant, wealthy, if slightly vulgar widow. But it wasn't out of selfishness. Surely not. Her father ought to remarry. He would be very comfortable with a woman of Mrs. Livesey's caliber.

But that was assuming he had an interest in the widow.

And the assumption was based merely on Angel's speculation.

Elinor was so distracted that she dropped and broke a snuffbox she had painted for the Dowager Marchioness of Trilby. So distraught that a bouquet of red and white roses with Lord Haversham's card, arriving while she helped Berthe prepare supper, had to be rescued from the rubbish bin by the older woman.

"Now what's this all about, Miss Elinor? I know we're an hour behind with supper, and we haven't seen hair nor hide of Sir Horace all day. But it isn't like you to be tossing flowers that certainly never did you any harm nor offered aggravation."

Elinor sighed. Berthe was quite correct, of course.

The poor roses couldn't help it that she detested the sender

"I'm sorry, Berthe. Just toss the card and take the flowers to your room. They'll look lovely on—"

"I'll do no such thing," Berthe interrupted firmly as she arranged the long stems in a crystal vase. "They'll go on your desk or on the credenza in the dining room."

"The dining room then, where everyone can enjoy them."

Everyone but me, Elinor thought, returning to the fricassee of chicken on the stove while Berthe carried off the roses.

At the rate trouble was escalating, Elinor had no time to look for another suitor. Haversham or Mr. Brigg, those were her choices. And she had no one to blame but herself. She had waited too long.

"Aunt Nellie?"

Spoon in hand, Elinor spun.

Angel said, "You're dripping on your gown."

"Because you sneaked in like a thief." Dropping the wooden spoon on a plate, Elinor snatched up a towel and dabbed at her skirts.

"I'm sorry if I startled you, Aunt Nellie. But Berthe won't tell me who sent the roses. She said to ask you. Are they from a beau?"

"No."

"Then who sent them?"

"Someone I'd prefer never to have to see again."

"Then why did he send them? Does he not know you dislike him?"

Elinor cocked her head. "My sweet, that is a very good question. Come to think of it, I doubt he sent them himself. He has a grandfather. . . ."

A grandfather who wasn't above meddling on his grandson's behalf.

As a certain daughter was not above meddling on her father's behalf.

"Aunt Nellie—"

A small warm hand slipped into Elinor's. She immediately paid attention. There was a certain note in Angel's voice that hinted at an imminent confession of sins.

"I drew Mary Wilton's cork today."

"You did *what*? No," Elinor added hastily. "Don't make matters worse by repeating such cant. We'll deal with your use of language some other time. Now I only want to know what happened."

"Mary said you'd never find a beau because you're long in the tooth and on the shelf."

Feeling barbarously and quite regrettably grateful to her niece for drawing little Mary's cork, Elinor said mildly, "No matter what the provocation, a lady must never ever engage in a fistfight."

Angel glowered. "You're *not* long in the tooth! You'll find a beau very soon, won't you, Aunt Nellie? You'll get married, and then I can pretend I have a mother and a father."

"You don't need to pretend, my sweet. You *have* parents."

"But not here."

Kneeling on the kitchen floor, Elinor drew her niece into her arms. Rashly, she wanted to promise to provide a substitute father just as soon as humanly possible.

If only Charles Collingwood weren't in as dire straits as she was herself. Angel would enjoy flying a kite with him.

And Angel's aunt would enjoy all kinds of activities permitted a married lady. . . .

Her precocious niece said, "I know you cannot marry just to please me. But isn't there anyone you like, Aunt Nellie?"

It was fortuitous that Berthe returned.

"The table is set, Miss Elinor. We may as well eat now since there's no knowing when Sir Horace will return."

Supper was a subdued affair, with Berthe providing the larger part of any conversation. Only when, with the baked apple dessert, the housekeeper introduced the topic of school, did Angel respond with animation. To voice indignation, as it turned out.

"We wrote an essay on 'My Family,'" she said. "And Mrs. Grimshaw tore mine up! And now I have to start all over again!"

"Upon my soul!" Berthe set down dessert spoon and fork with a clatter. "That's no way to treat a sensitive child I wish you'd told me when I came to fetch you, lovey. But never fret. Mrs. Grimshaw will have a piece of my mind tomorrow."

"Did Mrs. Grimshaw say why she tore up your essay?" asked Elinor.

"She said I mustn't lie about my grandfather."

Elinor's heart sank. Not for the first time that day. And the scent of the roses was giving her a headache.

Reluctantly, she inquired, "What did you write, Angel?"

"I described how Grandpapa planted that man a facer."

This time, Elinor did not bother to address her niece's use of cant terms. "What man?"

"The man who came to the flat door one evening, and Grandpapa asked me to let him in because you were in the shop and Berthe did not hear the knock. Grandpapa punched him because the man said he'd start bothering you if Grandpapa didn't listen. And Mrs. Grimshaw said I'm telling taradiddles because a gentleman has no dealings with a moneylender. But I asked Grandpapa after the man left, and he *said* it was the moneylender!"

Head throbbing, Elinor rose. "Perhaps it would be more suitable to write about the steamboat ride you and Grandpapa took."

"I did. And how Grandpapa played cards in the salon with the lady in the red dress. And the other one. Aunt Nellie! Can you believe it? She was painted even more than Mrs. Livesey!"

"How . . . fascinating." Elinor gripped the back of her chair. "Berthe, dear, would you help Angel with an essay Mrs. Grimshaw can accept? And please close up the shop. I have the headache a little and want to lie down."

"It'll be a pleasure closing the shop," said Berthe.

"Did I give you a headache, Aunt Nellie?"

"No, love." Elinor smoothed Angel's troubled frown with a kiss. "I think it started sometime this morning. Only I didn't notice until now."


In her chamber, Elinor felt guilty. Angel was her responsibility, not Berthe's. She should help her niece write an essay depicting a family acceptable at Mrs. Grimshaw's Academy for Young Ladies.

She should have a talk with her father. Painted ladies in the company of his granddaughter! And Abel Crisp, the moneylender. Punching him out, too!

When they owed eleven thousand pounds.

And Sir Horace losing more at cards. The interest payment. The rent.

Even Lord Woolwich, if he knew, would balk at such encumbrances and withdraw the heir he'd been dangling in front of Elinor's nose.

Not that she wanted Haversham.

Pulling the pins from her hair, Elinor sat down in front of the dressing table. The pressure in her head eased as soon as the heavy chignon at her nape loosened.

She reached for the Congreve matches. And stopped, arm outstretched, hand poised to close around the box.

Sitting quite still, she released her breath slowly. What a dissembler she was! A headache, indeed. As if she'd allow such a minor nuisance to drive her to her room. Lowering though it might be, she had best face the truth.

She hadn't been able to wait to get to her room because she wanted to light a match.

And not for the fascination of watching a scientific marvel. What she wanted to see was the magic of the previous night. The magic Charles Collingwood had, apparently, experienced as well.

Distantly, the tall-case clock in the shop struck eight times as Elinor doused the candle on the dressing table and, with unsteady fingers, lit a Congreve match.

She held the match high . . . and there it was, reflected in the mirror . . . the drawing room with crimson furnishings, the fireplace surmounted by white marble, an ormolu clock on the mantelshelf showing eight o'clock.

And there was Charles Collingwood, taking several quick steps toward her.

"I knew it!" The deep voice held satisfaction. Triumph, almost. "I knew I could make you return. I've been thinking about you ever since you dismissed me so harshly."

"I wasn't harsh. It was only common sense to part when nothing could be gained by further discussion."

"Are you always ruled by common sense, Miss Courridge?"

"If only I were! Was I not foolish enough to tell you that you might return if you still wished to see my father? Or to purchase matches?"

She saw the smile in his eyes, and did not remember joining him. But she was standing close to him, in that beautiful room.

"Where are we?"

"In my town house. Miss Courridge, in the park you said that above all we should deal truthfully with each other. I won't deny that I was infatuated with your sister. But it was you I admired. You never flirted but were always charming. You never teased but did not mind getting roasted when paint dappled your face or your hair."

He reached out, touching her hair, so lightly that she felt it no more than the brush of a gentle breeze. But it sent shivers of pleasure from her scalp to her toes. Or, perhaps, it was the sincerity and richness of his voice that affected her so deeply.

"In short, Miss Courridge, my admiration for you is of long standing." He paused. When he spoke again, his voice was even darker, richer than before.

"And it could easily develop into something stronger."

She saw no reason to cut him off or to shrink but stood quite still, her eyes never leaving his face. His hand slid beneath her hair, cupping the back of her neck. She should step away, but, instead, she leaned into the pressure of that warm palm that felt as if he hadn't been above hoisting a sail or two during his years at sea.

"What I wanted to, but had no opportunity to say in the park—Miss Courridge, our marriage would not be a cold, dispassionate marriage of convenience."

"No . . . I daresay it wouldn't." She was strangely breathless, found it difficult to think clearly.

"I would do anything in my power to make you feel a cherished wife. To make our marriage as rich and fulfilling as you would wish it to be."

"Yes . . . I daresay you would." Her gaze was still locked with his. She did not want to break the spell, but a tiny spark of reason prevailed. "The problem is . . . there cannot be a marriage."

His face clouded, and suddenly she was in his arms, his mouth claiming hers in a kiss that defeated reason and common sense. A kiss that melted every bone in her body, that heated her blood and made the world spin until she felt herself sink into the blackness of a swoon.

She struggled against the faintness, against the dark. She felt his hold loosen, his arms slipping, leaving her standing alone.

In the dark.

In her own bedchamber.

* * *

When she rose in the morning, Elinor was just as bemused as she had gone to bed. And as reluctant and, at the same time, impatient to see Charles Collingwood.

It should be impossible that a levelheaded woman of advanced years behaved so foolishly.

But, strangely, she did not feel a single one of those advanced years when she was with him.

And even stranger, she could not, as she went through the mechanics of her daily duties, think rationally about her meetings with Collingwood. She could not separate her feelings during the imaginary encounters from her reaction to him in the shop and in the park.

As if her feelings mattered when her selection of a husband must be made from two contenders. Edwin Brigg and Lord Haversham.

The memory of Collingwood's mouth claiming hers still lingered. The strength and warmth of his arms. The touch of his hand. . . .

She tried to imagine kissing Edwin Brigg but could only picture sitting in opposite chairs in a stuffy parlor furnished by his late mother, Brigg sipping something from his cellars, and she trying to hide her yawns behind the covers of a novel.

And the mere thought of being touched or kissed by the obnoxious Haversham was enough to make her snap one of the finest Cuban cigars the shop had to offer.

Horrified, but no more so than the footman sent for the purchase, she stared at the damage.

"Lud, ma'am! If Sir Horace weren't yer pa, ye'd be out on yer ear. That be a month wages or more!"

Elinor gathered her wits. Or, at least, attempted to

do so. It did not help that the morning passed, and much of the afternoon, without a sign of Charles Collingwood. Neither did it make her feel more competent to remember belatedly that his kiss had been pure imagination.

But she must still see him. She must know whether he had lit a match and saw her in its light.

The tall-case clock, her father's pride, carved in the likeness of a Highlander with bagpipe and swinging tartan, struck the half hour past four.

Elinor stiffened. The clock had struck eight times when she lit the match the previous night. The ormolu clock on Collingwood's mantel had also shown the hour of eight. If Collingwood saw her as she had seen him, had he also experienced the embrace? The kiss.

Had he felt her response?

Thank goodness she had no customer watching her face burn.

There was barely enough time to regain a semblance of composure before the street door burst open to a wild jingle of the bell, and Angel danced into the shop.

"Guess what, Aunt Nellie! I'm bringing a surprise."

"How nice. Is that why you are late? And where are your books? And where is Grandpapa?" Elinor caught her breath. "Surely he did not forget to meet you!"

" 'Course not. Can you guess what the surprise is? I'll give you a hint, shall I? It's not a thing. It's . . . ?"

Elinor heard footsteps approaching the door Angel had left open. Her father's irregular gait, and a steady, firm tread. A tread that once upon a time— ten years ago—had been very familiar indeed.

"Guess, Aunt Nellie. Quick!"

"Mr. Collingwood," Elinor said faintly.

"How did you know?" The child's face showed disappointment but instantly brightened again. "He's carrying my books, Aunt Nellie! He said a pretty girl should not have to carry books when an admirer is at hand. Does that mean he's my admirer?"

Looking past her niece, past her father just entering the shop, at the tall, sunburnt man with smiling dark eyes, Elinor said, "You had better ask him, my love."

But Charles Collingwood had a keen ear. "I am definitely an admirer, Miss Angel. And I shall be glad to carry your books as often as opportunity permits."

"How often is that?"

Charles Collingwood set Angel's satchel of books on the side counter. He looked at Elinor. "That quite depends on your aunt, Miss Angel. You see, I am her admirer, too."

Elinor grew warm under his gaze.

"Are you courting my aunt, Mr. Collingwood?"

"Indeed, he is," said Sir Horace, rubbing his hands. "And with my blessing."

"No," said Elinor. "He is not courting me."

Charles Collingwood only smiled. Sir Horace and Angel paid no heed at all to Elinor's protest.

Angel took a stance, one foot thrust forward so that a white stocking showed beneath the frill of her plaid wool gown, hands clasped behind her back, wide blue eyes raised gravely at Collingwood.

"Then you don't have to be my admirer, Mr. Collingwood. I want Aunt Nellie to have a beau all of her own. Will you be hers?"

"Angel!" Indignation and amusement warred in

Elinor's breast. "That's quite generous of you, I'm sure. But a beau is not passed from one lady to another."

"This one is very appreciative," said Collingwood.

"And I promise I'll never pester you about carrying my books if you marry Aunt Nellie."

"In that case—" Again, Collingwood looked at Elinor. "Miss Courridge, may I have a word with you in private?"

Elinor's heart was hammering. There was no purpose in private speech.

But there was!

She could not leave the shop.

What humbug!

"Stop dawdling, Nell." Sir Horace tried in vain to mask a look of smug satisfaction beneath a scowl. "He did ask my permission, if that's what's keeping you.

"In that case, Papa," Elinor replied with dignity, "you had best mind the shop. And Angel. Mr. Collingwood, if you will follow me?"


They faced each other in the rarely used, dark and chilly sitting room at the back of the apartment.

"Miss Courridge, will you marry me?"

"I cannot." The words were barely audible. As if she were some shy young thing, thought Elinor, dispirited. And irritated with herself . . . for wanting to be selfish. For wanting the man of her choice.

Much more firmly, she said, "You know I cannot marry you, Mr. Collingwood. Indeed, I must not."

"Then I am glad I pilfered a box of matches before coming upstairs." Watching her steadily, he lit a match with the sure precision of considerable practice. "I shall prove to you that you can—indeed, that you must marry me."

He held the match aloft, drawing her gaze to its bright flame.

"Miss Courridge, what do you see?"

Her eyes widened. "The crimson drawing room . . . the mantelpiece of white marble . . . the ormolu clock."

"What else?"

As if mesmerized, she kept staring at the warm light. "You."

"And I," he said, "see you with your hair down."

Suddenly she was caught in his free arm. His head bent toward her, blocking her view of the match. His mouth claimed hers, and she no longer needed the magical flame to experience the greatest magic of all. The magic of his touch. His kiss.

Collingwood released her abruptly, but only to toss the match, now burning dangerously close to his fingertips, into the cold grate. Immediately, he drew her into his arms again.

"Elinor." His voice was husky. "Must you have riches to be happy?"

"No." Surely it was impossible that a heart could burst with joy and, at the same time, shatter from despair. Yet that was how she felt. Tentatively, tenderly, she touched his face. Smooth shaven, yet with a hint of roughness. "With you, I could live in deepest poverty and still feel rich. But there are others I must think of. Others to—"

His mouth found hers again, muddling her thoughts, vanquishing reason so that she did not protest but responded with all the abandon so carefully shored for many years. Just once more, she would melt to his touch, feel her own passion kindle, taste his hunger and her own. Just once more.

She was gasping for breath when they drew apart.

"Now listen to me," he said, sounding just as unsteady as she felt. "I knew last night that I could not let you go. I lit a match. And I kissed you then, Elinor! And you responded just as you did now. With such warmth. Such fire."

"But last night—Charles, that was pure imagery!"

"It was powerful, like a waterway, a mighty river craftfully dammed, and suddenly bursting free."

She clung to his hands, afraid of the moment when she must let go.

"Elinor, did you not feel it, too?"

"I shan't deny it. But a mighty river . . . ?" She smiled, albeit shakily. "I thought it was infatuation, trammeled for years, and suddenly allowed to roam free."

"Infatuation? You? For me? But how, then, could you fail to recognize me? Elinor, that was a snub."

"How like a man to feel pique that I did not wear the willow for ten long years. But, in truth, I put you from my mind when you did not return after Melanie's wedding."

And, perhaps, already before then, when she had witnessed his infatuation with her sister.

She was clearheaded again. Knew she must put him from her mind once more.

Masking pain with firmness, she said, "Charles, this cannot be. You know it. And I know it. We simply must be sensible."

He broke into a sudden, boyish grin. "Believe me, I have been sensible all day."

He looked so cheerful that it cut her to the quick.

Was he quite unaffected by the inevitable parting of their ways? She felt betrayed, made a fool of.

"I've been to the City. Solved a great many problems. Elinor?" He cupped her face. "Are you paying attention?"

His voice was warmth enveloping her; the look in his eyes a caress cherishing her. She was a fool, indeed. If Charles hurt her, it was only because he had come back into her life far too late. Never because he made light of her feelings.

"I sold the estate, Elinor."

"Charles! Why?"

"Since it was encumbered, it did not bring much. But I have eleven thousand pounds for a certain moneylender. And two thousand to give us a start."

She stared at him.

His face clouded with concern. "Is it not enough?"

Lud! How difficult it was to fight the surge of hope. "Charles, you cannot do that! You mustn't sell **your** estate for me!"

"Why not? We won't be homeless. There's still the town house."

Her heart beat faster. Perhaps it was possible after all. Yes. Yes. She did not need much. Only Charles. A home.

"Charles . . . the town house. It has a crimson drawing room?"

"It does." He drew her closer. "And a fireplace with a mantel of white marble."

"An ornate gilded clock on the shelf?"

"You saw the room earlier, did you not? In the light of the match?"

"I saw it last night already. And the night before."

"I knew it!" His hands clasped her waist, swinging her high.

And she could not help smiling down at him, feeling young and giddy and not the least bit like a woman approaching thirty.

He caught her against his breast. "I knew we're meant to be together. Is it too soon—Elinor, would you call me a humbug if I told you that I have fallen in love with you?"

Words for the heart. For the soul. Words that lifted heavy dark clouds and let her spirit soar to the sky.

"No, I would not call you a humbug. Not when I look into your eyes and see the warmth of deep caring, when I see respect and admiration."

"And you, Elinor? Are you falling in love with me?"

"I am, if falling in love is wanting to be with you above any other. Sunny days or cloudy days. For always and ever." She smiled. "Happily ever after, or, as I often ended a fairy tale for Angel, quibbling and quarreling forever after."

"We shall live happily ever after."

"Indeed, we shall." She drew back a little. "But I am a sensible woman and must ask a sensible question. Charles, without the estate, how will we live? I fear the shop will not support—"

His laugh, though quickly suppressed, stopped her; made her frown at him.

"I beg your pardon, Elinor. But, no, I wouldn't be a great catch as a snuff or tobacco mixer. I shall be working for the Company. If it's all right with you?"

"East India Company?"

He nodded, watching her. "There's one drawback. It would involve a bit of travel. I want you with me.

But Angel, I understand, is not stout enough to weather hot climes."

It was Elinor's turn to laugh. "Did you look at her? Charles, she has been stout enough for years."

"Then why is the child not with her parents?"

When she hesitated, he gently touched her face. "You needn't answer. I think I know. I've seen Melanie. More to the point, I've seen her husband in his cups."

"It's sad, is it not? But, right or wrong, Melanie and I decided that Angel is better off with me. I did want to take her on a visit, only . . . it never worked out."

"Now it will."

Clasping her hands behind his neck, she kissed him. "Just wait till Angel finds out! She'll—"

"Yes, let us wait," he said firmly. "Do you realize, Miss Courridge, that this was the first time *you* kissed me? And it was scarcely more than a peck. Allow me to show you how it's done."

"I thought you'd never offer, Mr. Collingwood."

When later they returned to the shop, they found Sir Horace with Mrs. Livesey.

The widow blushed, gave Elinor a self-conscious look.

Before Elinor could speak, Sir Horace, limping toward her, boomed heartily, " 'Tis settled then? Well, I'm not saying you couldn't have done better with young Haversham. But Collingwood's a good lad. I'm satisfied, Nell. You've done all right."

"Thank you, Papa." Elinor turned to their landlady. "Mrs. Livesey, have you come about the rent?"

"No. Oh, dear me, no!" Again, the widow blushed and was quite uncharacteristically tongue-tied. "And

I never set out to . . . it wasn't on my mind to . . . what I mean is . . . Sir Horace, you shall tell your daughter."

But Sir Horace was occupied slapping Collingwood on the shoulder and assuring him that Elinor was good as gold, if a bit strong-minded and not one to mince her words.

"What should Papa tell me, Mrs. Livesey?"

"That he—Sir Horace, that is—" The widow drew herself up, took a deep breath. "Not to be mealy-mouthed, dearie—never was, and I shan't change good habits. The long and short of it is that before the month is out I'll be *Lady Courridge.*"

Elinor hugged her "But that is wonderful!"

"It is?"

Rubbing his stiff elbow joint, Sir Horace turned and gave his daughter a quizzical look. "Eh, Nell? What do you say? Now that I've got you fired off—"

"She said it's wonderful, Sir Horace!" Mrs. Livesey still looked astonished.

"A load off my mind," said Elinor.

She saw Angel standing in the curtained doorway at the foot of the staircase. There was an air of uncertainty about the child that made Elinor hurry toward her.

"My love, what's amiss?"

Angel hung her head. "I was right about Grandpapa courting Mrs. Livesey, wasn't I?"

"You were, indeed. They will be married soon."

"And you'll marry Mr. Collingwood?"

Charles had joined them. Placing a finger under Angel's chin, he tipped up her face. "Yes. Your aunt has agreed to marry me. Is it no longer what you want?"

"I do. Except—" Angel stepped back. "Except I forgot that Aunt Nellie wouldn't live here any longer when she marries."

"But neither will you," said Charles.

"I won't?" Wide blue eyes hung on his face. "Where will I be?"

"With us. In our house. And sometimes you'll pack your books, and your aunt will collect her sketchbook and pencils, and we'll go sailing the world."

"And Berthe?"

Charles glanced at Elinor for guidance and, when she nodded, said with a mock long-suffering sigh, "Berthe, too. Anyone else we should include?"

With a squeal, Angel launched herself against Charles, bounced off, and flung herself in Elinor's arms.

"Isn't it fabulous, Aunt Nellie? We're getting carried off by our knight in shining armor!"

# Rapunzel

# Chapter One

Once upon a time in London town lived a Knight of the Garter, Sir George Carmadie by name. Customarily a bottle-a-year man, Sir George was told one afternoon by the woman he loved that she detested his spectacles, did not love him and would marry someone else. To the amazement of his friends, the knight sought consolation for his aching heart and bewildered brain on the very evening of his disappointment by consuming, in one sitting at Watier's, his entire year's ration of spirits. Upon depleting the bottle and discovering that he could still stand, though admittedly not without a bit of wavering, Sir George tossed his hated spectacles to the floor, crushed them beneath his boot heel and blithely announced to all that he would walk himself home.

"And I am doing admirably well at it too," he told himself contentedly. "I am not certain where I am, but I have not fallen once, not so much as stumbled, and something will look familiar soon if only I keep on walking. It is this dratted fog," he muttered, squinting myopically. "It insists upon tattering all about me and obliterating everything. Abominable. And wet."

It was so wet, in fact, that it at last occurred to Sir George's befuddled brain to look up to see if it was raining. It was and quite steadily. "Blast," he grumbled, swiping at his eyes with fisted hands. "All I need. Lost in the fog and drenched clear through. As if I am not miserable enough now that Ariel has thrown me over for that dandy, Blanchard!"

He shivered and pulled his greatcoat more closely about him. He set his booted feet to walking forward again. And then he halted so abruptly as to come near to knocking himself down. A square, hulking edifice poked out of the fog directly before him.

Thunderation! It looked like the White Tower! Sir George rubbed at his eyes and stared. How the deuce did he come to be standing before the White Tower? By Jove, and how had he gotten past the yeomen warders to be wandering about the Tower of London at all? Try as he might, Sir George could not remember entering the Tower grounds. But he ought to remember and he ought to have been challenged by the warders too. "I say," he called, his voice echoing eerily through the night. "Anyone here?" But the only answer was the rain pelting down around him and the rustling and calling of the ravens among the White Tower's crevices.

Sir George shrugged deeper into his greatcoat and peered around him. He could make out very little through the rain and the fog and the darkness. But it was definitely the White Tower before him. And a tower of the oddest proportions stood directly beside it, too. A round, extremely narrow tower with a sloping, pointed top. "Ought not be here," he muttered, glaring at the thing. "Wrong." He had brought Ariel to view the lion and the jewels and to stroll about the green only last week and there had been no tall, narrow tower with a sloping, pointed top beside the White Tower then. At least, he could not recall such a tower in such a place.

"The White Tower," he muttered to himself. "The Bell Tower, the Lion Tower, the Bloody Tower, Wakefield. . . ." He ticked the entire list of them off on his fingers, fuzzily attempting to remember where each one stood and to imagine what each might look like looming out of the fog.

"I am correct," he mumbled. "This tower does not belong here. Not at all. It was not here last week, and it makes one extra besides." He closed his eyes and opened them again, slowly, to see if perhaps the odd tower were a result of his mad drinking bout and would disappear. But it remained, peering mysteriously down at him through two enormous, rectangular windows that lay just beneath the pointed, sloping roof. "Where the deuce did this come from?" he muttered, taking a step back and staring upward.

His inebriated curiosity engaged, Sir George approached the narrow tower and made his way around it. "There is no door!" he exclaimed quite loudly as he completed the circumference and discovered himself staring back up at the two great eyes that glowed down at him through the fog. "But there are lamps alight up there. How the deuce did lamps get lit if a person cannot get into the place to light them?"

And then he heard the voice of an angel singing sweetly and purely through the inhospitable night.

"Come sweet knight with face so fair
With emerald eyes and midnight hair.

Thou art brave and bold; I trust in thee.
Come rescue me. Come, love, rescue me."

Sir George Carmadie's jaw dropped. The thoroughly delicious voice floated down from beyond the tower windows. And it was singing about him!

Not that my face is fair, he thought. I am brown from the sun and my nose tilts at the tip and I wear spectacles. But my eyes are green and my hair is black and by gawd, I am a knight!

Sir George straightened his greatcoat, doffed his beaver and combed his fingers through his hair. He was just about to hail the owner of the angelic voice when he heard hooves pounding in his direction. Thinking it to be one of the warders and not wishing to be escorted from the grounds before he could discover the singer of that remarkably sweet song, Sir George dashed on unsteady legs into the deepest shadows of the White Tower. "Will not notice me here," he muttered as he huddled against the cold, wet stones.

From the depths of night, out of rain and fog, like a demon rising from the smoke of Hades, a magnificent black stallion swirled into the bit of light that dwindled down from the two windows at the top of the slender tower. The beast reared and snorted and pawed at the air. As it settled, a slight figure in a wildly billowing cloak jumped to the ground and gazed upward. Amidst a rising wind and flashing lightning and a teeth-rattling clap of thunder, a distinctly feminine voice called upward. "Rapunzel! Rapunzel, let down your hair!"

What the deuce? thought Sir George confusedly, and then his weary emerald eyes opened wide. "By Jove!" he gasped.

From one of the tower windows a braid of golden hair tumbled to the ground below. The figure in the billowing cloak seized one handful after another of that marvelous braid and scurried up it, leaping, at the last, nimbly in through one of the windows.

"Jupiter!" exclaimed Sir George under his breath. "Jupiter!"


"I cannot believe, Aunt Eustacia, that you have come all the way here on a night like this," said the young lady, busily tugging her hair in out of the rain. "And look, you have left poor Handy to stand about without the least bit of shelter. He will certainly die of a congestion of the lungs."

"Nonsense," replied Eustacia, doffing her cloak and going to stand near the fire. "He is a magical steed, Rapunzel, given to me by my Uncle Solomon the Lord of the Winds. He is not like to die from such a mundane ailment as a congestion of the lungs. However, if you insist," she murmured, and crossing back to the window, she snapped her fingers in the direction of the stallion. Instantly it poofed from sight, leaving a silent, awe-filled, and completely unnoticed Sir George Carmadie staring at the spot where it had stood. "There. I have sent him to the stables. Now you need not worry. I have come with news, Rapunzel."

"What sort of news?"

"The very best sort. My expenditures for the renting of the mansion in Grosvenor Square have not been in vain. Your Cousin Guinevere is to be married, my dear. She has brought an earl up to the mark this very evening!"

"Oh, Aunt Eustacia, how wonderful!" exclaimed the young lady, her blue eyes alight with joy. "At last Guinevere has found a gentleman to love!"

"Do not," growled the small, slender lady with a shake of her bright red curls, "speak to me of love. I warn you, Rapunzel, love has nothing to do with anything. Girls. Always droning on about love. Bah! Fetch me a brandy, girl, and we shall have a quiet coze before the fire, eh? I am in a mood to tell you all about it, Rapunzel. But I must return to Grosvenor Square before the servants there rise, so I have not a great deal of time."

Hastily pinning up her heavy braid, Rapunzel stepped down to the chamber below. Scooping up a snifter and the crystal brandy decanter, she hurried with them back into her Aunt Eustacia's presence. The first glass she poured disappeared down Aunt Eustacia's throat in a matter of moments. The second glass took a bit longer. The third glass managed to linger for the length of several minutes before it, too, was consumed. And the fourth glass of amber liquid sloshed wildly about with every expansive gesture that Rapunzel's aunt made as she described in a victorious voice the gentleman who had succumbed to Guinevere's multiple charms.

"He is a lord, my girl, and rich as Croesus, too! I shall never be forced to economize again. Things will be very different from now on, you will—hic— see. And he is the perfect buck, too! No doubt thinks to marry the girl and keep her secluded in Hertfordshire while he carouses about London. Ha! Men! What beetlebrains they all are. As though Guinevere does not wish to be secluded in a veritable castle in Hertfordshire with all of her husband's money to hand and not one fear of his learning the first thing about where any of it goes."

"Do you think he will, Aunt Eustacia? Abandon Guin in the country and give her money as well?" asked Rapunzel.

"Most certainly. He will abandon her because he is a buck of the first head. And he will allow her his money because he will feel guilty for abandoning her. And you and your Aunt Glennis and I shall join Guinevere the instant the gentleman departs for London. We will make a perfect little nest for ourselves at Margate Hall, and I shall rule the entire countryside."

"Oh, Aunt Eustacia, you have always wished to rule an entire countryside. It is your dream come true, is it not?"

"I am so giddy about it all that I am almost inclined to drop my assault against Lord Harry and let him be," murmured Eustacia. "I shall have no need for his paltry little property now. But no, I do not think I shall let him be. He has always been deserving of my wrath and now he shall continue to feel it regardless."

It did occur to Rapunzel, as Aunt Eustacia's eyelids fluttered sleepily, that she had never heard mention of a Lord Harry before. It was seldom that Aunt Eustacia mentioned anyone but herself. But that was neither here nor there. They were going to move. That was the important thing. They were going to move to a Hall in the country! At last Rapunzel was to be free of the tower. At least, she thought it meant that she was to be free of the tower. As her Aunt Eustacia began to snore before the fire, Rapunzel began to pace excitedly about the chamber.

\* \* \*

Once Sir George Carmadie had convinced himself that there had actually been a horse, by getting down upon his hands and knees and searching the soggy ground for hoofprints, he unsteadily regained his feet and blinked hazily upward. He glimpsed a play of shadows in the lamplight and a certain flickering as if there were a fire up there as well as lamps. He stood staring for the longest time and at one point, when the wind had ceased to whirl about his ears for a moment, he thought he heard a most tremendous snore.

"What the deuce?" he mumbled to himself over and over. "What the deuce?" And then he went to rest his shoulders against the White Tower so that he could stare upward more comfortably. In less time than it took him to sigh, he was asleep, his tall, lean form sliding slowly to the ground.

When he awoke the sun was already high in the sky, the rain had ended and the ravens were cawing raucously. Steam rose from his pantaloons and from his greatcoat. And his boots, stretched far out before him, were covered in mud. He blinked his emerald eyes in weary disbelief and struggled to gain his feet. His head pounded and his stomach churned and he reached out to steady himself by placing one York tan gloved hand against the wall of the White Tower. Dazedly he squinted about him. "What am I doing here?" he muttered. And then a vague memory of the other tower—the tall, slender tower with the sloping top—came to him and he looked about gingerly to see if such a thing actually existed. It did not. "Never drink again," Sir George mumbled, attempting to stand without the White Tower's support. "Never drink spirits again so long as I live. Ought to have known better. Home. Go home. Forget it ever happened. It did not happen," he reminded himself then. "I was foxed. Dreamed the entire thing."

Sightseers had just begun to dribble into the grounds as Sir George made his head-throbbing way past two of the warders and tramped uncomfortably off in the direction of his digs in Little Charles Street. He had not the least idea what he would say to his man, Wiggens. His pantaloons were in the most despicable state and it was doubtful whether his greatcoat could be saved from the fire or not. He sincerely hoped that it could. He had purchased it from Weston only two weeks ago to impress Ariel and—

The thought of Miss Ariel Browne, her eyes as soulful as a forest fawn's, tugged at Sir George's heart and he sank deeper into gloom. He sighed heartily, drawing the attention of a number of passersby. How could Ariel have dismissed him so cruelly, so heartlessly? Had he not paid her court for two full Seasons? Had he not written her poetry and sent her posies and waltzed with her in the sancto sanctorum of Almack's? Indeed he had. And when he had at last screwed his courage to the sticking point and requested her hand in marriage, had she not told him yes? Indeed she had. The banns had already been read. Twice! But that did not matter, Ariel had informed him yesterday. They must still be read the third time, and they would not be. She would notify the parson at once.

"Deuced Blanchard," Sir George muttered. "She

prefers that deuced Blanchard. Because he is an earl, that is why!" But he knew that was not why—not the entire reason at any rate. Not only was Lord Blanchard an earl, he was rich and extremely handsome to boot, a combination that must win out over a mere knight with an adequate income who wore spectacles that Ariel despised and who possessed but one house, and that in Dover.

"But I could sell the house in Dover," Sir George grumbled, his boots turning at last into Little Charles Street. "I could sell the house in Dover and purchase a manor house somewhere more fashionable. Except, I cannot afford to purchase a manor house somewhere more fashionable. I should never get enough for my house to do it. And I cannot afford to keep an establishment in London just for the Season either, which Blanchard can and does." With another sigh, Sir George climbed the three steps to Mr. Bainbridge's boardinghouse, shuffled in through the front door and made his way dismally to the second-floor front.

"I was about to set off in search of your body," announced Wiggens, his arms filled with freshly pressed neckcloths, as Sir George entered the chambers. "Thought you had gone down to the Thames, pressed a pistol to your head and pulled the trigger."

"What? Huh? Pardon me, Wiggens. What did you say?"

"Nothing, Sir George. Merely that I was worried about you."

"Well, I had a most interesting day yesterday, Wiggens. And an interesting evening as well: I downed an entire bottle, I think, at Watier's. I do not remember quite. And I do not feel quite the thing either," Sir George added in a murmur, setting his hat upon the vestibule table and tugging off his gloves. "I did attempt to come home, but I got lost in the fog."

"Lost in the fog?" Wiggens cocked a disbelieving eyebrow. "Between Watier's and here, Sir George?"

"Yes, between Watier's and here and I do not wish to discuss it further. I mean simply to apologize for any worry I may have caused you." Sir George shrugged out of his greatcoat and hung it upon the wooden tree in the vestibule.

"It is because you were not wearing your spectacles," offered Wiggens, following his employer into the parlor and setting the pile of neckcloths upon the sideboard.

"No, it is because I was totally foxed."

"No, it is because you were not wearing your spectacles," insisted Wiggens. "I have told you time and again that you cannot see well without them. You ought to put them on, Sir George."

"It is those blasted spectacles that have ruined my life!" exclaimed Sir George angrily, slumping down into the chaise longue and holding his head with both hands. "Ariel has always hated that I wear spectacles. And so last evening I smashed them to death upon the floor at Watier's!"

Wiggens stared at his gentleman with a deal of sympathy. And then, as gently as possible, he knelt down to remove Sir George's muddied boots. "Well, you shall need to be fitted for a new pair then," he murmured consolingly. "Truly, Sir George, there is not a woman in the world worth such agony as this."

"You know?" cried Sir George, sitting up straight,

his feet crashing to the floor. "You know about—about—What the deuce! Is it in the newspapers already?"

"No. Do not begin jumping about now, sir, or your head will ache all the more for it. Lie back as you were and rest. It is merely that the lady sent back the ring you had given her and it was I received it from her messenger."

"I expect Blanchard gave her a bigger ring," mumbled Sir George, leaning back again into the chaise. "I expect he gave her a ring covered in diamonds and rubies and emeralds."

"I expect he did," agreed Wiggens, lifting the boots by the tops between his thumb and index finger and carrying them, held out before him, onto the little landing beyond the kitchen door. "I expect he gave her a ring the size of Westminster Abbey," Wiggens muttered, knowing Sir George could not possibly hear him. He dropped the boots and turned back inside. "I expect that dandy gave her papa a most handsome settlement as well. You are better off, my lad, without that one. She did not love you. Not one bit. Out to sell herself to the highest bidder and nothing less. But you will discover a young lady someday whose heart is true and then you will never think of Miss Browne again."

# Chapter Two

Three weeks to the day after Miss Ariel Browne had broken his heart, Sir George Carmadie attended a ball. Wiggens duped him into it. Before Sir George so much as noticed, he was stuffed into white shirt and buff breeches, white waistcoat and midnight blue jacket, white neckcloth and high white collar and black dancing shoes. In a veritable whoosh, he was out the door and into a hackney and carried to Berkeley Square.

As he stood in the reception line, Sir George pondered the thing. As he bowed over the dowager Lady Margate's hand, he could not but think that Wiggens had taken great advantage of him and his lingering listlessness. As he congratulated his old schoolmate, Margate, upon his approaching nuptials, he winced at the thought of his own ill-fated plans and cursed Wiggens for sending him out into Society when he was not at all ready to go. And as he took the hand of Margate's intended into his own and placed a chaste kiss upon the back of it, he told himself that he would strangle Wiggens the very moment that he arrived back at his own rooms.

Sir George was not primed to attend a ball. Especially, he was not primed to attend an engagement ball. He did, in fact, never wish to hear the word engagement again. But here he was at the Margate mansion in Berkeley Square, crushed amongst a throng of the couple's friends and acquaintances, about to celebrate the engagement of the present Earl of Margate to Miss Guinevere Longfellow.

Why is everyone an earl but me? Sir George thought with an enormous degree of self-pity. And why do earls never require spectacles? Had I been an earl and free of spectacles, Ariel would be upon my arm this very evening. But no, I must be a paltry, myopic knight. And even though my heart is broken to bits and will likely never be whole again, I am still expected to go on as though nothing has happened. No doubt, now that I have appeared at this affair, people will expect me to dance as well.

"You are going to dance, are you not, Sir George?" asked Margate's mama with a smile as she came up behind him a quarter hour later. "You have been wandering about like a little lost lamb for the longest time, my dear. We are depending upon you to do your duty by the young ladies, you know. There are always so many more young ladies at the balls than there are gentlemen."

"Yes, well, I expect," sighed Carmadie, attempting not to notice the distinct look of pity in the dowager Lady Margate's eyes. She knew that he had been jilted. Of course she did. Everyone knew by now. Ariel's engagement to Lord Blanchard had been announced in all of the society columns only Wednesday past.

"Oh, and there is just the young lady to whom I ought to introduce you!" exclaimed the dowager happily. "She is shy and has not set one foot upon the dance floor this evening. She requires a very kind sort of gentleman to lead her out, I think. And you, sir, are the very kindest of all my son's acquaintances. She is Miss Longfellow's cousin, Miss Garden. Come," the dowager urged, taking Sir George's hand in her own and leading him as though he were a child of six across the chamber and past any number of people who knew that Ariel had turned him away in favor of an earl without spectacles. She led him smack up before the most beautiful young lady he had ever seen.

"Miss Garden, may I present Sir George Carmadie who has professed an earnest desire to lead you onto the floor for the very next dance."

"Oh!" gasped the young lady whose hair was as golden as summer sunflowers and whose eyes were as bright as a bluebird's wings. And then she curtsied quite properly and looked up into Sir George's spectacles.

Sir George took the spectacles off immediately and tucked them into his pocket. "Good evening, Miss Garden," he said politely.

"Good evening," she replied and then drew him a few paces forward to introduce him to her chaperone, a tiny lady with flaming red hair, most of which was tucked up beneath a ludicrous purple turban. "Aunt Eustacia, may I present Mr. Carmadie," she said in a most musical voice.

Sir George thought to correct Miss Garden as to his title, but decided it was not worth the effort and instead merely bowed to the chaperone and forced himself to smile as well.

"Come to dance with the girl, eh?" mumbled the lady. "Well, I expect one dance will do her no harm."

Unfortunately the dance proved to be a contre-danse and, try as he might, Sir George could not see Miss Garden's face clearly at all. Had it been a waltz and she standing quite close within his arms, he would have done very well for himself, but so far apart as the dance kept them, he had to squint his eyes most violently to bring her face into focus.

"Am I doing something wrong?" asked Miss Rachel Garden in the barest whisper as they came together.

"No, not at all," managed Sir George. "Why do you ask?"

"Because you are glaring down at me so sternly. Do forgive me, Sir George, but I have never danced with a gentleman before and if I am mistaking the steps, you must tell me."

"Never danced with a gentleman?"

"Never with a gentleman. I have only danced by myself in my little room. You must tell me what are the steps I am mistaking and I will dance more properly or—or—you may lead me back to Aunt Eustacia. But I hope you will not do that, because then she will scold me and lock me away again."

"Lock you away?"

"Yes. I ought not to be out at all, but Cousin Guinevere begged and begged for me to be allowed to attend, and since it is such a very special occasion Aunt Eustacia at last agreed that I might come. Why, now you are practically scowling. Am I truly making such a muddle of this dance?"

"Not at all," declared Sir George, a smile replacing the scowl as he at last decided that he had gone quite mad and that Miss Garden had not intended, just now, to imply that she was generally locked away like some prisoner, but rather that she was as yet a schoolroom miss and had not made her comeout into Society. "It is merely that I cannot see you well without my spectacles," he offered with a smile, "and so I am squinting. I could have seen you well enough had this been a waltz."

"You must put your spectacles on," declared Miss Garden.

"No, I shall muddle through without."

"You are ashamed to wear them," Miss Garden said accusingly. "That is why you took them off so hastily when we were introduced. But you ought not to be ashamed. Spectacles are most becoming."

"Becoming what?" asked Sir George facetiously.

Miss Garden laughed and her laughter was music, and the music drove all thoughts of spectacles, earls, Ariel and Ariel's betrayal from Sir George Carmadie's mind.

It proved most puzzling to him. So puzzling, in fact, that Sir George pondered deeply over it as he strolled through the night toward Little Charles Street. Miss Garden's laughter was not like music. It was music. And her voice, when she spoke, was music. And it was music that he had heard before, too. But that could not possibly be, because Miss Garden was a schoolroom miss and had never been out in Society. Had she not said as much? Miss Garden. Miss Rachel Garden of the tantalizing tresses and the brilliant blue eyes and the face of an angel. He had danced with any number of other young ladies and then, late in the evening, he had petitioned Miss Garden for a second dance. Her chaperone had eyed him most curiously but had given consent in the end and, for the second time that evening, Sir George Carmadie had felt free of sorrow and free of self-pity and free of Ariel.

He had not expected to remain at the ball for longer than an hour. He had remained until three o'clock. Even after Miss Garden's chaperone had sent the girl off, Sir George had remained, thinking of the pretty miss and sipping champagne. Of course, he had been careful not to sip too much champagne because the memory of his entire bottle night still plagued him and he had not the least wish to suffer through such a night and such a day following again.

Remembering that night, Sir George came to a standstill and gazed about him. This night there was no fog, no rain and he was not foxed. This night his new spectacles were on his nose; there was a bright three-quarter moon; and he knew precisely where he was. "Jupiter!" he exclaimed, staring at the White Tower as it hunched hungrily in the moonlight before him. And then he turned to discover the tall, slim tower with the sloping, pointed top peering down at him from a great height. "I am dreaming. This is a dream," Sir George told himself. "I cannot possibly be at the Tower when all I did was set out to stroll from Berkeley Square to Little Charles Street. The Tower ain't even along the way!"

Miss Rachel Garden in her plain cotton nightrail sat before her looking glass and tugged her brush through her long, golden tresses. She detested her hair. It was so very long that it pooled about her on the floor and she was forced to lift it in strands onto her lap in order to untangle all the ends. And it was heavy, too. Especially when it was pinned up, which it must always be, because she could not possibly walk about with her hair trailing behind her along the floor from chamber to chamber. Thank goodness that Aunt Eustacia had been in such a very kind humor and had poofled it into a more manageable length for Guinevere's ball. Thank goodness that Aunt Eustacia had let her attend Guinevere's ball! The very thought of the ball brought a tingling and a shortness of breath, and a most giddy feeling around her heart.

"That is because *he* was there," she sighed wistfully. "My knight. I never once imagined that *he* would attend Guinevere's ball!" The joy of gazing up and discovering him there before her had set her poor heart to lurching. It had been such a surprise! To this very moment a most delectable thrill of happiness and certain victory coursed through Rachel's veins. But then a most sinister chill crawled up Rachel's spine and set her to shuddering. What if Aunt Eustacia should suspect that Sir George is the one? But she will not. "I introduced him to Aunt Eustacia the very first thing," Rachel told herself. "Aunt Eustacia would never expect me to introduce to her the very gentleman who is to be my rescuer."

No, she would never expect me to do that, decided Rachel, attempting to drive the chill of fear from her bones. Aunt Eustacia thinks that I am a perfect featherbrain and a compliable gudgeon and she would never suspect me of such brazen effrontery as to introduce to her the very gentleman who will be her downfall. And I was most careful not to use his title, too, she reminded herself. If I had introduced him as Sir George and not as Mr. Carmadie, then Aunt Eustacia might well suspect. But I did not. I did everything quite properly. And giving her reflection a confident nod, Rachel set her brush upon the vanity table and began the onerous task of braiding her tresses.

"But I did never once imagine that he would be so very handsome," she whispered. "From the first time that Aunt Glennis saw him in her crystal ball and told me of him, I did never once imagine that his hair would be so very thick and dark and curly, or that his nose would have such an appealing tilt at the tip, or that he would have those particular eyes— eyes that can stir a woman's very soul. Oh, he is so much more than I ever dreamed!" A smile wound its way around her lips and across the dimples in her cheeks and upward into her eyes. And continuing to braid her hair, she began to hum. And once humming, she began to sing.

"Come sweet knight with face so fair
Of emerald eyes and midnight hair.
Thou art brave and bold; I trust in thee.
Come rescue me. Come, love, rescue me."

Sir George who, in disgust, had just begun to stomp off across the verge toward home, stopped and spun around at the sound of that haunting song. "By Jupiter," he murmured, recognizing the voice at once, "it is Miss Garden singing." With long strides he hurried back to the base of the tall, thin tower and gazed upward. Now he realized why Miss Garden's voice had seemed so familiar to him. He *had* heard it before—he had heard it calling to him on that dreadful night when he had known for certain that Ariel had left him.

"Miss Garden," he whispered hoarsely upward. "Miss Garden," he called with a bit more volume.

And then he brought himself up short. What sort of a Bedlamite was he to be shouting Miss Garden's name upwards at two windows in a tower—a tower which did not exist, no less?

"Well, it cannot exist," he told himself severely. "It must be a figment of my imagination. And even if it does exist—which it does not—how can Miss Garden be in such a place when she went off in a coach to the town house Miss Longfellow has taken for the Season? I am mad. That is what. I am stark, raving mad and it is all Ariel's fault. I have been crossed in love and my mind and heart have devised a madness between them to keep me from the real world.

But Miss Garden existed in the real world. Most certainly she did, for had he not danced with the young lady—twice? Most certainly he had. And he had enjoyed every moment of it, too.

Sir George stepped into the shadows of the White Tower and, sighing, lowered himself to the ground and leaned back against the cold stone, staring up at the tower which he was quite certain did not exist. Perhaps I did drink too much champagne, he thought dismally. Perhaps that is why I see this tower and hear Miss Garden's sweet voice singing to me. I shall simply sit here and wait for this odd illusion to fade away. And when I see it fade, then I will know for certain that I am sober and I shall never take another drink of anything resembling spirits ever again. And tomorrow morning I shall send Miss Garden a posey and I shall pay her a morning call, and I shall prove to myself that she resides at present in Grosvenor Square with Miss Longfellow and her aunt and cannot possibly be singing to me from some deuced tower.

Miss Garden. As exasperated as he was with himself for having fallen into the depths of this very confusing illusion, the thought of Miss Garden calmed him and made him smile. Truly, he had expected to have the most dismal time this evening and yet Miss Garden had made it enjoyable. Of course, she was merely a schoolroom miss visiting her cousin and so he must not become too enamored of the girl. But certainly her aunt would not take exception to his visiting Miss Garden once or twice. Perhaps he might take her to view Week's Mechanical Museum or to spend an afternoon at Madame Tussaud's. Any number of young people not yet in Society visited such places as those when they came to London.

Sir George doffed his hat and set it down beside him and stared thoughtfully at his shoes. Surely her aunt would not be discomposed to have him come knocking upon the door, offering to take the girl sightseeing. Surely not. And then he had the most marvelous idea. He would petition his mama to let his sister, Tess, accompany them. Tess would be delighted. She was a good deal younger than Miss Garden—Tess being merely ten—but not even the sternest of guardians could suspect him of anything less than great goodwill in offering to show Miss Garden about London with such an innocent as Tess at his side.

"By Jove, that is just what I will do," declared Sir George. And just as he reached for his high-topped beaver and prepared to stand, to ignore the rattle-brained tower and to stroll off home so that he might arise early enough to visit his parents and gain permission to take Tess about on a sight-seeing tour, the sound of hooves pounding across the verge in his direction stopped him completely. His hat dangled from his hand. One knee rested upon the ground and the other not. He turned his head in the direction of the sound and saw, galloping at him through the moonlight, the same black stallion that he had seen the last time. Sir George stood. He took his spectacles off and peered at it. He put his spectacles back on and peered at it again. Still it came, hooves flying, head tossing, mane and tail flying in the breeze. "Jupiter!" murmured Sir George. And not at all confident that this stallion and its rider were also a figment of his imagination, he stepped back into the shadows of the White Tower and watched in silence.

With a great deal of bravado—neck arched, front hooves flailing in mid-air—the stallion came to a halt before the narrow tower and a tiny woman in long skirts with a turban upon her head that glittered oddly purplish in the moonlight hopped lithely to the ground. Like a beetle encased in an iridescent shell, she skittered to the grass beneath the tower windows and, in a voice that seemed all too familiar to Sir George, she called upward, "Rapunzel! Rapunzel, let down your hair."

Sir George pressed his shoulders against the cold stone and stared at the woman as a long, wide braid came shuddering over one of the windowsills and thwacking down the side of the tower to land at her feet. She clutched at the braid and scuttered up it like a rat up the rope of a ship. Once she had reached the window she hopped inside and then the braid began to be tugged up and inside as well.

Dazed, Sir George wandered out from the shelter of the shadows and approached the horse that stomped and snorted beside the tower. By Jove, but that tiny woman had looked like Miss Garden's Aunt Eustacia! Of course it could not be because there was no tiny woman, not truly. She, too, must be a figment of his imagination. And if she did not exist, then she could not possibly be Miss Garden's aunt who was likely home in bed in the town house in Grosvenor Square this very moment.

Inching his way closer and closer to the bit of blood and bone which had ceased to stomp about and now eyed him warily, Sir George began to murmur sweet phrases. "Good boy, pretty boy, what a fine beast you are, my lad."

The horse pricked its ears and snorted.

"Yes, that's a boy. There is not a thing to fidget about. No one is going to hurt you." Ha! thought Sir George. As if anyone could hurt such an animal. Have his skull kicked in first, I should guess. And then he was running one York tan gloved hand down the beast's neck and combing his fingers through the beast's mane, and the stallion was nuzzling at his pockets. Looking for an apple, no doubt, thought Sir George.

Looking for an apple? He was standing beside the stallion, stroking it and combing his fingers through its mane and it was nuzzling him in search of an apple? By Jove, the horse and rider were not imaginary! They were as solid as he was himself! Which meant that the tower was real and the long braid was real and the voice—the voice made of music—was real as well! Was the tiny woman actually Miss Garden's Aunt

Eustacia? Was the sweet voice of song actually Miss Garden herself?

Sir George gasped at such a staggering thought. Real! All of it as real as he was himself! "She will lock me away again," Miss Garden had said as they danced, and he had pondered it, wondering if her aunt might be cruel and lock the girl into her chamber at times. Had Miss Garden meant that her aunt would lock her away in a tower? This very tower? Sir George stepped back and stared up at the lighted windows. Then he stepped forward and took a fistful of silky mane into his hand. Then he heard the tiniest snap—and poof! the horse was gone. The horse was gone and Sir George was standing beneath the tower with a handful of nothing.

# Chapter Three

The following evening, just after midnight, Sir George made his way to the Tower of London under his own power and by his own design. He heard the ravens flutter and call as he attempted to keep to the shadows. He dodged past two warders without once being noticed and made his way by a circuitous route to the White Tower. And there beside it stood the slender, round tower as proud and tall in the moonlight as the main mast of a man-o'-war. For a moment Sir George thought that he would shout aloud in triumph, but then he remembered the warders and did not. Pushing his spectacles up further on his nose with one knuckle, Sir George made his way cautiously around the base of the tower. He had been correct from the first about that, too. There was no door to be seen anywhere.

He returned to the shadows of the White Tower, rested his shoulders against the stones and stared upward at the two lighted windows. Was Miss Garden up there? And if so, how did she come to be locked in a tower? Sir George Carmadie's brow creased in thought. Since the very moment last evening when the stallion had disappeared, his mind had been gnawing upon the possibility that necromancy, sorcery, even witchcraft did, indeed, exist. Almost, this morning, he had confided in Wiggens, hoping to get a realistic opinion upon the subject. But then he had thought better of it just as he had, throughout the day, thought better of seeking his father's advice and his mother's and his brothers' and his friends'. The only person he had asked for an opinion had been his sister, Tess. Now he wondered if he ought not to have spoken to someone beyond the age of ten. But Tess had assured him that magical towers did exist and that witches were real and that there were, indeed, fairies in the bottom of some people's gardens. And she had told him what he ought to do, too, because—

"You are meant to be her hero, Georgie!" Tess had exclaimed. "You would never have seen the tower else. That is how it works. Only her hero may see her wretchedness and rescue her. Oh, Georgie, you are to be a real hero at last!"

Sir George grinned as he remembered Tess' excitement and the considerable awe in her eyes. A real hero at last. Never mind that he had used his considerable acumen and intellectual abilities to uncover and thwart a plot intended to bring down the Prince Regent. Forget that he had been knighted for his display of wisdom and courage and loyalty to England. All that, apparently, was as nothing when compared to the magic of the tower and the young lady confined within. Only now was his heroism a viable possibility in Tess' eyes.

But was Tess, in all her innocence, correct? Was Miss Garden under a witch's spell and he destined to rescue her? Well, there was only one way to be certain. He would call up to Miss Garden. On Tess' advice, he would be certain to use the precise words that he had heard the woman use. With a shake of his head at his own foolishness but a hope in his heart that it was not foolishness, Sir George Carmadie stepped out into the moonlight beneath the tower windows and looking upward called out, "Rapunzel! Rapunzel, let down your hair."

Sir George's heart leaped up into his throat and came near to choking him as a thick, glorious golden braid tumbled down the side of the tower. He did not believe for one moment that he could climb it. He was not, after all, a tiny woman but a full-grown gentleman of considerable weight and it was a braid of hair—a thick braid to be sure—but not a ladder for the likes of him.

"Magic," he whispered to himself then, seeing Tess' awe-filled eyes before him. "This is magic and I am a part of it. I am Miss Garden's hero. I can climb the braid. I am meant to climb it." And giving his spectacles another nudge up his nose to be certain they were securely in place, he stepped up and took the braid in his York tan gloved hands and began his ascent.

By Jove, he thought, as he paused a moment to look back and saw the ground a considerable distance below him. By Jove, but Tess was right! And all doubt leaving him, he continued his climb until he reached a window and, with a shift and a tug and a lurch, hurled himself through it and into the tower itself.

Miss Rachel Garden, with a gasp of delight, threw her arms about his neck and kissed his cheeks and his chin and his slightly tilted nose and at last his lips with the utmost abandon. "I knew!" she cried as she pulled back from him the tiniest bit and gazed happily up into his eyes. "I knew you would come! I knew you would! You are not afraid of Aunt Eustacia!"

Sir George, beaming from the hearty reception but also thoroughly discomposed, reached up and took Miss Garden's arms from about his neck, then made to remove his spectacles.

"No! Do not! There is not the least need, Sir George," declared Miss Garden. "I think you look most impressive with them on. Truly I do."

"Do not fib, Miss Garden. Ariel spoke plainly to me about them. 'No woman can discover a gentleman to be her romantic ideal when she gazes into his eyes and sees naught but her own reflection gazing back at her from bits of glass.' That is exactly what she said and I expect she is correct."

"Ha!"

"Ha?"

"Indeed. Whoever this Ariel person is, she does not know the very first thing about love, you may believe me. If a bit of glass keeps her from seeing what is in those flashing green eyes of yours, then she does not love you, not one penny's worth."

"No, she does not. She told me that in no uncertain terms. What are you doing, Miss Garden?"

"I am tugging in my braid."

"Tugging in . . . ? Oh! Of course!" And with a most bemused smile, Sir George leaned over the sill and began tugging upon the braid as well.

"How did you know to come now?" asked Miss Garden as she let him pull the braid upward and began to gather it about her and pin it up in loops upon her head.

"I made certain that your aunt would be attending

a fete in honor of Margate and Miss Longfellow. I thought it would be best not to attempt to reach you unless I knew her to be occupied elsewhere. Is—is your aunt a—witch, Miss Garden?"

"Indeed. But she is not truly my aunt," Miss Garden replied as the last of her braid entered through the window. "She is a genuinely powerful and selfish old witch who once lived in the dower house upon my papa's estate. Come and sit down, Sir George, and I will fetch you some wine and—"

"No, I rather think not, Miss Garden. Tea, perhaps."

"Oh, tea? Well, if you think you would rather. It will only take me a moment," and with that Miss Garden, sticking the last few pins into her braid, was tripping merrily out of the chamber.

Sir George listened to the whisper of her slippers descending a flight of stairs and then stared about him at the perfectly round room into which he had climbed. It appeared to be a parlor. Upon the wall opposite to the windows, a coal fire burned upon a respectable hearth. Before the hearth a wing chair upholstered in a lavender brocade sat quite properly and beside it a cherry-wood cricket table which held a lamp. To his left was a matching settee with a long, low table before it and to his right, a framed looking glass hung upon the stone. Below the glass, a vanity table of rich mahogany completed the sparse but exquisite furnishings.

Curious, Sir George crossed to the doorway through which Miss Garden had exited and poked his head out into the corridor. There was no corridor. Only a staircase leading downward. Sir George nodded. The tower was quite as narrow as it appeared from the outside. There was only space for one chamber and the staircase upon each floor. He wondered how far Miss Garden had been forced to descend to the kitchen to make tea. Most likely all the way to the ground floor or possibly below that.

Ought to have settled for the wine, Sir George thought. But then he shook his head. No. No more wine. Never, as long as I live. Look what spirits have gotten me into.

"It is all because of my mama's craving for the witch's lettuce—her rapunzel to be exact. That is why Aunt Eustacia calls me Rapunzel when no one is about and why she has given me the last name of Garden. She finds it to be exceedingly humorous."

Sir George sipped his tea and cocked an eyebrow.

"Very well, I will tell you all, but it is not particularly interesting," sighed Miss Garden. "When Mama was increasing she developed the most insatiable craving for rapunzel and the only place that it grew upon the estate was in the witch's garden. Because the dower house was across the park and could be seen from the drawing room window, Mama could not get the rapunzel from her mind. She could practically see it growing there and every night she begged my papa to go and fetch her some."

"And he did," murmured Sir George.

"Yes, over and over again until it became most obvious to the witch that someone was stealing her lettuce. And one night she lay in wait for Papa and, when she caught him pulling the rapunzel from her garden by the light of the moon, she threatened to do the most dire things to him and to Mama."

"He ought to have thrown her out of the dower

house and closed the estate to her," muttered Sir George.

"No, he could not do that. He was powerless against her. And he was truly terrified. He loved Mama very much, you know, and wished to keep her from all harm."

"Wished to keep himself from all harm, if you ask me."

"No! I will not believe such a thing of my papa. Aunt Eustacia says the same and laughs, but it cannot be so." Miss Garden's angelic countenance crumpled into an ominous frown and the very first thought to enter Sir George's mind was that he should very much like to kiss that frown into a smile.

"I am mistaken then," he said instead. "And so what happened next, Miss Garden?"

"Well, well, Papa promised to give me to the witch as soon as I was born. And he did. And I have lived with her ever since."

"In this tower?"

"No, not always. I lived in other places when I was young."

"You must have lived in your father's dower house, do not you think, if that was where the witch resided? Why did she leave the dower house? Did your papa at last discover a way to drive her out? And if he could do that, why could he not get you back?"

Miss Garden stared at Sir George, her most expressive lips formed into a tiny O. "I never thought to ask that," she said at last. "I know it is very important for Aunt Eustacia to discover a place to stay now. That is why she is so delighted that Guinevere has made a match. We are all to live on the earl's estate in Hertfordshire while he lounges about in town. And Aunt

Eustacia plans to spend his money, too. She says that Lord Margate is so very rich that she will never be forced to economize again."

"You are all to live on Margate's estate? You and your aunt and Miss Longfellow?"

"Yes, and my Aunt Glennis. She is Guinevere's mama."

"Does Margate realize?"

"No, I do not think that Guinevere has told him. She truly loves him, you know, and will not believe what Aunt Eustacia says—that he will abandon her and come to town alone. Guinevere believes that Lord Margate will wish to be forever in her pocket and to have her forever hanging upon his sleeve."

"Yes, well I should think so. Anyone may see from the way he looks upon her that Margate has lost his heart. I doubt he will abandon your cousin to her own resources and I doubt, too, that he will allow your aunts to rule him. Margate is not likely to let anyone rule him, not even a witch." Sir George set his teacup aside, rose from the settee and began to pace around the small chamber. "I expect you had the whole of this tale about your father and mother and yourself from the witch?"

"Yes."

"And you believe every word of it?"

"Yes. Do not you believe it?"

"No. For one thing, why would your mama or any woman develop a craving for lettuce? Increasing or not, lettuce? No, my girl, I hardly think so. Ices from Gunter's perhaps or raspberry tarts or gingerbread— my mama developed the most frightful craving for gingerbread before Tess was born—but rapunzel? I think not. And if your papa was not born a poltroon, he would never have made such a dastardly bargain. And for your mama to go along with it—to give up her child—it is plain balderdash.''

Sir George ceased his pacing and dropped down again beside her upon the settee. He placed a finger beneath her chin and gazed down into her wide blue eyes. "Do you not know your papa's name? If he was in possession of an estate, it is likely he was a country squire or a lord. If I could get in touch with him—''

"I do not know his name.''

"Never mind then,'' murmured Sir George. "I will do whatever is necessary to free you from this witch, Miss Garden. You must only tell me how to go about it.''

"You do not know?'' asked Miss Garden on a tiny gasp.

"I have not the foggiest notion.''

"Oh! I thought—that is, you are my knight and—''

"You have not the foggiest notion either, have you, Miss Garden?'' Sir George sighed, taking one of her hands into his own and placing a kiss upon the inside of her wrist. "Never mind, my dear,'' he said kindly, clasping her hand in both of his. "You must only go on as you have always done and be certain not to mention that I have come to visit you, and I will begin to study over the matter, eh? I will come up with something. I give you my word upon it.''


He was not only her knight and her hero, Sir George Carmadie was the gentleman she loved, and the gentleman she would marry, too! Miss Rachel Garden pressed the inside of the wrist he had kissed to her cheek and closed her eyes. Even now she could see the promise of love flashing in his emerald eyes.

How could anyone—anyone—have turned such a gentleman away for someone else as Guinevere had told her Miss Ariel Browne had done? Well, she would not turn Sir George away, never in a thousand years. She would love him and marry him and bear his children. They would grow old together amidst grandchildren and great-grandchildren. And even when his midnight curls had turned to pure silver and he had become crotchety with age, she would love him still with all her heart.

"Rapunzel! Rapunzel! Rapunzel, you dratted little featherbrain, let down your hair!"

Rachel jumped to her feet. Aunt Eustacia! How long had she been calling? She sounded dreadfully put out. Tugging at her braid, causing hairpins to fly in all directions, Rachel hurried toward the windows. With a haste born of panic, she flung her hair over the sill and it descended with a twirl and a bounce and a thump directly down upon Aunt Eustacia's head.

The witch staggered under the force and the weight of it and, grumbling, seized the braid and made her way upward. "Of all the stupid gudgeons I have ever known, you are the very stupidest!" she cried, hopping in over the sill. "Where have you been, girl? I have been standing about shouting your name for the past quarter hour. Never mind. Never mind," she growled as Rachel opened her mouth to explain. "Just go and fetch me the brandy, girl. I have had a severely distressing night. Fetch me the brandy and then take yourself off to your bed."

Rachel, who had been pulling her braid hastily inside, reached the end of it just as Aunt Eustacia collapsed into the wing chair before the fire. Hurriedly twisting it up onto her head, she searched the floor for enough hairpins to keep it there and then veritably flew down the staircase to the witch's chamber and scampered back up again with brandy decanter and snifter in hand. As she skidded into the little parlor she noticed with the most sinking feeling that Aunt Eustacia had sat up very straight in the chair and was sniffing at the air around her.

"Someone," the witch declared, "has entered this tower. Who was it, girl?"

Her cheeks red from her mad dash down the staircase and up again, Rachel set the brandy decanter and the snifter down upon the cricket table. "I cannot think, Aunt Eustacia, what it is you mean. No one has been in this tower in all the time I have lived here except yourself and Aunt Glennis and Guinevere and me."

"Someone," growled the witch, "has been in this tower this very evening, my girl. A gentleman. I can smell him."

"Well, of all things!" cried Rachel, assuming the most featherbrained countenance she could manage. "A gentleman? How dare a gentleman come here when he is not invited. Where is he, Aunt Eustacia? I shall give him a piece of my mind, I shall. Of all things, to sneak into our tower! We must search him out at once and ring a peal over his head."

The witch stared at her, and sniffed the air, and stared again. "There is no possible way that a gentleman can have entered this tower without your having allowed him to climb your hair, Rapunzel."

"Are you quite certain, Aunt Eustacia? Because I did not. I have spent the entire evening washing and drying my hair. I did drift off to sleep before the fire, but I am quite certain—" Rachel turned about and took a sniff at the air herself. That was it! She could smell it too. Sir George's scent. The faint odor of frankincense and cloves. "Oh, I did never tell you. Cousin Guinevere presented me only yesterday with the most wonderful gift. It is called Imperial water. It smells so much nicer than rain water in my hair, do not you think?"

"Gudgeon," grumbled the witch, ceasing to sniff at the air and opening the brandy decanter instead. "Imperial water is exactly what I smell. It is not water, Rapunzel, for washing in. It is a scent that gentlemen wear. I cannot think what possessed Guinevere to present you with a bottle of it. You both have nothing but air between your ears. And Guinevere has the most air of all!" she added with a sneer. "Takes after her mother. You will never believe it, Rapunzel. She claims she loves that dratted lord and that he loves her and he will not go off to London and allow me to take over his estate. Damnation, but I shall not only be forced to carry on against Lord Harry, I shall be forced to win. If I do not, I will never have a proper countryside to rule."

# Chapter Four

Sir George settled into one of the chairs at Gunter's and, sending the waiter off to procure two lemon ices, smiled across the table at his little sister.

"Did you do it, Georgie?" Tess asked eagerly.

"Yes, last night, just after midnight."

"And did it work? Did you get into the tower? Was your Miss Garden there?"

"Yes, yes and yes," grinned Sir George.

"Oh! Oh, Georgie, I was correct! I knew I was!"

Sir George chuckled at the look of pride in her eyes as the waiter set their ices before them. "What else, I wonder, do you know about witches, Tess?" he asked once the waiter had departed.

"Any number of things. Why?"

"Because if I am to be Miss Garden's hero, I must know a great deal more than I do now. I have no idea how to free her from the tower, you see, nor can Miss Garden think how it is to be done. I thought that if I told you what Miss Garden told me about herself, that you might have some suggestions as to how I am to go about rescuing her." Sir George spooned a bit of ice into his mouth, swallowed and then launched into the tale Miss Garden had told him the night before.

"Rapunzel?" asked Tess in awe. "She is under a witch's spell all because her mama craved rapunzel?"

"So she says, but you must remember that it was the witch herself told Miss Garden the tale and I think she lied."

"You think it is a Canterbury tale?"

"Indeed I do. Does it make a difference, Tess?"

The Honorable Miss Theresa Amelia Carmadie frowned thoughtfully beneath the brim of her poke bonnet. She wiggled the tiniest bit in her chair and stirred the melting ice in her dish with her spoon. Then she sighed and frowned some more. "It may make a difference," she offered at last, "but it may not. Witches often lie. Can you not just take a ladder with you next time and help Miss Garden to climb down from the tower?"

"It would take at least six gentlemen to carry a ladder that long—if I had a ladder that long—which I have not. And she cannot climb down her own hair, Tess," murmured Sir George with some frustration. "The witch did free her for Margate's ball, but Miss Garden says she poof!ed her from the tower to Berkeley Square. And I cannot poof! anyone anywhere."

"Why can she not?" interrupted Tess excitedly, the spoon in her hand bouncing up and down before her.

"Why can she not what?"

"Why can Miss Garden not climb down her own hair! Then you need not carry a ladder at all. All you would need to carry, Georgie, is a scissors!"

"A scissors."

"Yes, Georgie. You cut off her braid and tie it to something very strong and then you both climb down her hair to the ground!"

"A scissors," murmured Sir George. "A scissors."

Wiggens puzzled over it for the longest time. Why would Sir George, dressed for a comfortable evening at his club, discover himself to be in need of a scissors to carry about with him in his coat pocket? And why had he been whistling so merrily when he left the flat? And why had he not once in the past two days so much as mumbled the name Ariel?

Abruptly Wiggens gulped and blanched. No, it could not be. But Sir George had been so thoroughly crushed by Miss Browne's cruelty and he had been acting oddly for any number of days. And only this afternoon he had gone out of his way to take his baby sister to Gunter's. And now—now he had strolled from the flat at the hour of eleven with a scissors in his pocket, declaring that he was off to play some macao at Watier's. He was not off to play macao at Watier's at all! He was off to put an end to his grief and himself by jabbing Wiggens' scissors through his poor broken heart! "Oh my dearest heaven!" exclaimed Wiggens, running his fingers through his hair. "Oh my dearest heaven!" And in a matter of moments, Sir George Carmadie's man was jamming his hat upon his head and dashing from the flat.

"Where could he have gone?" Wiggens mumbled under his breath as he searched the street for a hackney. "I ought not to have hoaxed him about putting a pistol to his head. I ought not to have done. Where could the lad have gone?" And then a hackney appeared and Wiggens flagged it down and bid the driver carry him to Bolton Street. Because he may have gone to Watier's, Wiggens thought. He may have gone to Watier's as he said, not to play macao, but to bid his friends farewell. And it is not that long since he left home. Perhaps I can come up with him at Watier's.

The hackney driver obligingly waited at the curb as Wiggens approached the doorman to inquire if Sir George Carmadie might be within. The doorman, not recalling Sir George's entrance that evening at all, but noticing a hint of panic in Wiggens' eyes, sent one of the waiters in search of the knight. It was but a matter of a five-minute wait before the waiter returned with a tall, broad-shouldered gentleman following in his wake.

"Wiggens? What is it?" asked the gentleman. "Come inside and speak to me. You are pale as a ghost." Captain Jeremy Carmadie seized his brother's man by the elbow and escorted him into a small antechamber at the front of the establishment. "Come, Wiggens, you may confide in me. What has you apucker? Has Georgie landed himself in the briars? You know I will help him in any way that I can."

Captain Jeremy Carmadie was the third youngest of the five Carmadie brothers and six years older than Sir George. He had the black Carmadie curls and the green Carmadie eyes and like all but one of his brothers had not yet stumbled into Parson's Mousetrap, though innumerable female hearts prayed daily for him to do so. "Wiggens," he insisted, "if George is in trouble—"

"Oh, Captain Jeremy," Wiggens gasped, his determined self-control for a moment failing him. "Oh, Captain Jeremy, Sir George has gone off to put a period to his existence!"

"What? Georgie? Never, Wiggens."

"Yes, yes he has. He must have done. He left the flat only a bit ago whistling and saying he was bound for Watier's. And—and—he took my scissors with him!"

"He took what?"

"My s-scissors. Tucked them away in his pocket very carefully. Adamant, he was, that he must have them. Planning to stick them into his heart, he is. I have considered it from all sides and I cannot find any other reason for him to have taken my scissors. I have got to find him. I have got to stop him."

"Yes, well, it is all because of Miss Browne, is it?"

"Yes, sir. So I think. He has been in despair over Miss Browne for weeks and weeks. And now, suddenly tonight, he has gone off whistling and with my scissors tucked in his pocket."

Jeremy Carmadie could not quite bring himself to think that of all the things available to him, his little brother would choose to end his life by means of a scissors; but the true panic written large upon Wiggens' face could not be denied and Wiggens, after all, spent a good deal more time with George than anyone.

"Is that your hackney waiting at the curb, Wiggens?" he asked abruptly. "Good. We shall both climb in and search the streets for Georgie, eh? You will keep watch upon one side and I upon the other, and the moment we see him, we shall hustle him into the coach and carry him back to Little Charles Street and you and I both will set about coddling him and determining what is to be done."

Rachel waited at the open tower window, her elbows resting upon the sill, her chin resting upon her fists and a smile hovering about her lips. She watched him as he approached through the shadows and, before he could so much as look upward and murmur Rapunzel, her braid was flowing down the side of the tower for him to climb. "Oh, but I have missed you," she declared, tugging him inside. "I thought you would never come. It has been the very longest day of my life."

"And the longest day of mine," Sir George replied, tossing his hat onto the settee and taking the girl into his arms and hugging her gently against him. "I thought the night would never come." And standing back from her the slightest bit, he kissed her tenderly upon the lips, then wrapped her in his arms again. "I think, Miss Garden," he whispered in her ear, "that I have quite lost my heart to you. Until the evening we met, I was certain I had no heart to lose, that it had been broken beyond repair. But I was mistaken. It beats with a passion it has never known right this very moment. And there is something—something I wish to ask of you. No, I shall not ask it until you are free of this dratted tower."

"What? What do you wish to ask?"

Sir George stared down at her through his spectacles, studying her every feature—the glorious golden hair, the bluebird bright eyes, the sweet upturned nose, and those oh so tempting lips. Then he shook his head, loosed his arms from around her, and set about pulling up her braid. "No, do not bother with your hairpins," he said as she began to gather the braid into loops. "You shall not need to pin your hair up for a long while once you are free."

Miss Garden looked at him with the most puzzled expression.

"I am going to cut it," Sir George explained, pulling the scissors from his pocket. "Snip the braid right off and tie it to something heavy like—like—the settee—and then you are going to climb right down out of this tower with me."

The smile that lit Miss Garden's face was dazzling.

"Come sit down over here by this little vanity," Sir George instructed, "and I shall begin. I am not adept at cutting hair, mind you, but I will do the best I can to leave you enough to comb into some fashionable style. Any number of young ladies are wearing their hair short these days."

Miss Garden's reflection was smiling thankfully upon him from the looking glass as Sir George, nibbling at his lower lip, nudged his spectacles up further on his nose and took scissors in hand. Then he coughed nervously, set the scissors down upon the vanity table, stomped across the room and returned with one of the lamps. He set the lamp down so that the light would shine fully upon her, picked up the scissors again, swiped at his brow with the sleeve of his jacket and exhaled loudly.

Miss Garden giggled.

"I should not giggle if I were you," murmured Sir George, a large dash of good humor sparkling in his eyes as he met her gaze in the looking glass. "There is no telling what sort of muddle I will make of this."

"I may be required to purchase a wig," giggled Miss Garden.

"Oh, I do hope not," declared Sir George heartily. "My Aunt Theodora wears a wig."

"Do not you like your Aunt Theodora?"

"Yes, but her wig always flops about whenever she moves. Sometimes it slips left and sometimes right and sometimes straight down over her eyebrows. When we were children we used to beg to be allowed to remain in Aunt Theodora's company for as long as possible and we would make a game of guessing which way it would slip next. Tess still loves to watch it."

"Tess is your sister?"

"Yes. My only sister. And merely ten," murmured Sir George, once again nibbling at his lower lip and turning his full attention to scissors and hair. "Well, I'll be dashed," he mumbled after a moment, and he held the scissors up before him and studied them closely. "Perhaps they require sharpening."

"Sharpening?"

"Well, they are not cutting at all. You simply open them and put the hair in between and close them, correct? I mean, there is no great secret to scissors when it comes to hair? They are used in the same fashion upon hair as upon anything else."

"Perhaps you are attempting to cut too much at once," offered Miss Garden. "It is a very thick braid. Perhaps you ought to cut just a few strands at a time."

Sir George nodded, nudged his spectacles up and

set about cutting just a few strands at a time. "By Jupiter!" he exclaimed after his third attempt at it. "This scissors is positively useless. It will not cut even the thinnest of strands. I cannot think but it is in terrible need of sharpening. Look, Miss Garden." And with that, Sir George bent down until his reflection was beside Miss Garden's in the looking glass, lifted one of his own curls from his brow and snipped it clean off.

The two turned to stare at each other. "It is Aunt Eustacia's spell," whispered Miss Garden, her eyes misting with tears. "My hair cannot be cut because of Aunt Eustacia's spell."

"Do not cry, m'dear. We will think of another way."

"But what other way can there be?"

Sir George had not the least idea and was strongly considering another discussion with Tess, but he could not bear to see tears standing, unshed, in Miss Garden's eyes, and so he ceased to consider anything at all and instead sat down beside her on the very edge of the little vanity bench and put a comforting arm about her shoulders. With his index finger he tickled her beneath her chin, and when she looked up at him, his eyes were aglow with humor.

"What?" Miss Garden asked with the tiniest sniff. "What is it you are thinking?"

"I ought not to tell you," grinned Sir George. "You will likely think me a frightful dastard and never speak to me again."

"No, would I?" asked Miss Garden, her lips twitching upward. "I cannot believe it. Tell me what you are thinking."

"Only if I may call you Rachel and you will call

me George. I cannot bear to tell my thoughts to someone as proper-sounding as Miss Garden."

"George," smiled Rachel. "And you must tell me this very moment before you burst into guffaws and cannot catch your breath to tell me at all."

"It is merely that—that another method of rescuing you has just now entered my most fertile imagination, Rachel. And to do it, we need not cut your hair at all."

"What? What do we do?"

"Well, you simply sit upon the windowsill."

"Yes?"

"And I take the very end of your braid and tie it to the leg of the settee."

"Yes?"

"And I move the settee to the window directly behind you, and then you jump."

"I jump?" asked Rachel.

"Indeed. Of course, I shall attempt to keep ahold of the braid so that it pulls up short and you do not hit the ground directly."

"I would not wish to jump and hit the ground directly."

"No. It will be much better if you dangle while I slowly lower you the rest of the way."

The very picture of herself dangling by her braid from the tower window brought the merriest laughter from Rachel. Sir George joined her in it. It was precisely what he sought, to drive the tears from her eyes and to renew the hope in her heart.

"Oh, you are a dastard," Rachel laughed, pounding her fists against his chest playfully. "To dangle me from my own window by my own hair. What an idea!"

"But it might well work, Rachel. It might. If, of course, I could get your braid unknotted from the settee leg once I had lowered you all the way to the ground. I am excessively good at tying knots, but not quite so adept at untying them."

"Wh-what would you do if you could not untie my hair?" gasped Rachel, attempting to subdue her laughter, but laughing even more at the thought of herself absolutely tied to the tower by her hair.

"Well," offered Sir George, pretending to give the situation the deepest consideration. "I expect that the best thing would be for me to toss the settee out of the window after you. That would work. Provided, of course, that when you landed, you had enough hair to move out of the way so that the settee did not land on top of you."

"But how would you get down, George, if myself and my hair were already upon the ground?"

"Ah, now that part is the easiest of all."

"It is?"

"Yes, my darling girl, it is. I would climb upon the sill and jump down, landing upon the settee and bouncing from there into your arms. You would not mind if I bounced into your arms?"

Rachel reached up and drew a slow line down his cheek to beneath his chin and then back up to his lips. Her laughter gone now as well as her tears, she twisted her fingers into the curls at the nape of his neck and drew him slowly to her. Her lips caressed his with a softness and a sweetness and a longing that sent an explosion of love through Sir George all the way from the top of his head to the soles of his feet. And then she snuggled against him, resting her head against his chest and wrapping her arms about his waist. "I would never mind if you bounced into my arms, George," she whispered. "You may bounce into my arms at any time and I will welcome you. But it would break my heart in two if ever you should choose to bounce out of them again."

# Chapter Five

"Where the devil have you been?"

"What?" Sir George came close to jumping straight up out of his boots upon the threshold to his own parlor. "Jeremy? What the deuce are you doing here? It is past two."

"I know what it is past, George. I have been keeping track of the hours since eleven when Wiggens came in search of you at Watier's." Jeremy Carmadie pushed himself up out of the chaise longue in which he had been dozing and set about lighting another of the lamps. "Jupiter, what happened to your hair?"

"My hair?"

"Yes. There is a great chunk missing right at the front. Someone pull it out for you?"

"No." Sir George could not help but smile at that thought. "Cut it off. Accident."

"You cut it off by accident? I vow, George, you have the oddest accidents of any brother I know. Do you remember the time old Bessie tossed you over her back with her horns? I do not know one other gentleman with a brother who got himself tossed by a milch cow. Come in and sit down and make yourself at home."

"I am at home, Jeremy," pointed out Sir George, beguiled by his brother's unexpected presence.

"Yes, so you are. And relieved I am to see it, too," replied Jeremy, strolling across the room to light another lamp which stood upon the sideboard and then taking a moment to pour himself a brandy from the decanter that stood there. "Drink, George?"

"No, thank you. I have sworn off the stuff."

Jeremy Carmadie harrumphed loudly.

"I have, Jer. I am strictly a tea and coffee man these days," murmured Sir George, divesting himself of hat and gloves and tugging at his neckcloth as he flopped down upon the sopha and planted his feet upon the low table before it. "Not that I am not pleased to see you, but what the deuce are you doing here? I had thought you to be still at sea."

"Came ashore this very afternoon. Stopped in to see Mother and Father and Tess. Dined with them, as a matter of fact. Then wandered over to Watier's to see who else might be in town. Season, you know."

"Yes, I know."

"Well, no sooner do I get to enjoying myself, but along comes a waiter in quest of you. Says that your man is waiting at the door. Something urgent. Well, I knew you were not in the club, so I went to tell Wiggens so. I vow, George, I have never seen Wiggens so pale and panicked. Thought to discover you cold and dead somewhere with a scissors through your heart, he did."

"What?" Sir George could not believe his ears.

"Indeed. He and I have spent the last three hours hacking about town in search of you. We have been everywhere, let me tell you. As far as Whitehall, and out to Cheapside and through every one of the parks."

"Cold and dead with a scissors through my heart?" chuckled Sir George. "Why? Why would Wiggens think such a thing?"

"Because, you dolt, you left the house with a scissors in your pocket. And Wiggens, knowing you wore the willow for Miss Browne, conceived the notion that you had gone to end it all."

"And you believed him?"

"Well, no, not actually. But I could not conceive of any reason for you to go off with a scissors in your pocket. And I was aware of your parting from Miss Browne, you know. Mama wrote to me about it. I will show you the letter someday. You will never believe that Mama could know some of the words in it, much less how to spell them. Where did you go, Georgie?" he added, flopping back down into the chaise.

"To the Tower."

"What? In the middle of the night?"

"Sneaked past the warders."

"Why?"

"I cannot tell you that. You will think I am gone mad."

"I have thought you mad from the first day I saw you all wrinkled and red and wailing in Mama's arms."

Sir George tossed his neckcloth across the back of the sopha and grinned. "The lady I love is imprisoned in a magical tower upon the Tower grounds and I am attempting to free her," he announced somewhat gleefully and the look that arose upon his brother's face sent him into whoops.

\* \* \*

The following night as the bells of London town struck twelve, Miss Rachel Garden peered hopefully out from her tower window. Her Aunt Eustacia had gone off once again to chaperon Guinevere. Oh, thank heavens for Guinevere! thought Rachel. She has gotten herself engaged at precisely the right time. Aunt Eustacia would always be around else and my George would never have the least opportunity to rescue me. Then she blinked her eyes in disbelief and blinked them again. Strolling toward her across the verge were what appeared to be three gentlemen chained together and two of them looked like George.

"It is a rope we borrowed from Jeremy's vessel," Sir George called up to her as the gentlemen came to a halt beneath the tower windows. "Jeremy is captain of His Majesty's Frigate *Talisman*. Oh, this is my brother, Jeremy, and my man, Wiggens. Gentlemen, Miss Garden. It took three of us to carry it, Rachel. Thickest rope I ever saw. At any rate, I am going to bring one end of it up and tie it off and Jeremy is going to hold it steady at the bottom while you descend. Once you are safely down, I will climb down myself."

Rachel nodded and smiled and lowered her braid down to him as Sir George positioned a great loop of the rope over his shoulder. "I told you," he whispered to his astounded brother and an agog Wiggens. "And she is truly the most wonderful girl in all the world, too."

Sir George made his way cautiously up Rachel's braid. He was forced to adjust the lie of the rope upon his shoulder from time to time so that it would not pull him off balance. When at last he reached

the top, Rachel helped him safely inside. As he lowered the rope from his shoulders, she gave him a
most welcoming kiss upon the cheek and grinned.
"My hero," she smiled, and then kissed him again.
The two then set about moving the heavy settee close
to the windows, and Sir George tied the rope in two
half-hitches around one of the thick mahogany legs.

"Now," he smiled, kissing the tip of Rachel's nose,
"on to the sill you go, my dearest. You must face me
and hold tightly to the rope with both hands. And
do not look down. Jeremy and Wiggens are below to
keep the rope from wobbling."

Rachel mounted to the sill, turned and knelt. She
took the rope in both hands. Then she inched slowly
backward. But no sooner did her legs clear the sill
and she begin to lower herself than the entire tower
began to quake, sending the settee and Sir George
and every piece of furniture in the parlor tumbling
madly about. Rachel, clinging to the rope, was
whipped into space and then thrown back against the
tower and then whipped into space again. Sir George
picked himself up from the floor and stumbled and
tumbled and lunged back in the direction of the window and over the settee, diving for the sill. Urgently
he stretched downward until he could grasp Rachel
by her upper arms. In such an awkward position it
took all of his strength to pull her back inside the
window again while the tower continued to weave
and shake and tremble around them.

"This will be the wretched gentleman who forgot
his scissors!" rumbled an angry voice from nowhere
and yet everywhere as George and Rachel fought to
keep from rolling off the settee and across the floor.
"This will be Rapunzel's knight, no doubt!" And in

a burst of smoke and a flash of lightning, Aunt Eustacia appeared before them.

"Forgot your scissors, my lad, and the feather-brained girl did not so much as think to hide them!" cried Eustacia. "Did you not know that I would guess how a scissors came to be here? How dare you, Rapunzel, attempt to escape me! And how dare you, sirrah, presume to outsmart me! I am Eustacia Adrianna Nightwing. I have never been outsmarted in all my life! And I will not be outsmarted by the likes of you!"

Sir George, at last gaining his feet as the tower subsided to a minor trembling, tugged Rachel up and encircled her with his arms. "You mistake me, ma'am, for whatever poltroon allowed you to steal Rachel in the first place. I shall not slink away at the mere roar and witless prattle of a witch."

"Mere roar and witless prattle, is it!" bellowed Eustacia, setting the tower to pitching madly once again. "I will show you, sirrah, what is mere roar and witless prattle!"

"Aunt Eustacia, do not," pleaded Rachel. "I shall send him away. I shall refuse ever to see him again."

"Too late! Too late for that!" shouted the witch.

"I should think so," declared Sir George. "I love Rachel, and I will never allow her to sacrifice herself to a hag on my account. You may believe that. I have sworn to rescue you from this harpy, Rachel, and rescue you I shall."

"Hag? Harpy? Me?" Eustacia's bray came near to breaking Sir George's eardrums and he winced with the pain of it.

Dangling from the rope midway up the tower, Jeremy Carmadie struggled to keep his purchase. He had begun to climb the very moment he had recognized that his brother was in serious trouble. Now, the sound of Eustacia's caterwauling sent stabs of fear deep into Jeremy Carmadie's soul. Below him, battling with all of his might to keep the rope taut, Wiggens' lips began to move in silent prayer as he listened to the angry screaming of the witch. With anxious eyes, Wiggens watched as Captain Carmadie began again to inch his way up the swaying rope. Twice more he crashed against the bricks of the tower as it lurched and tilted.

"I will show you, sirrah, who is a hag and a harpy! Rescue Rapunzel? Bah! Rescue yourself, if you can!" And with that Eustacia raised her hand and snapped her fingers in Sir George's face, sending him soaring against the wall even as Rachel flew from the protection of his arms and completely disappeared. "The girl is banished!" screeched the witch. "Find her if you can, Sir Knight!" And on a trill of ear-piercing, evil laughter, witch and tower alike vanished, sending Sir George and Jeremy plummeting to the earth and Wiggens staggering backward as the rope plunged down onto the verge before him.

"Sir George, Captain Jeremy," Wiggens cried once he had dropped the end of the rope and regained his balance. He ran forward to where the two brothers lay close beside each other in the moonlight and knelt worriedly between them.

"I am all right, Wiggens," groaned Jeremy, sitting up groggily. "I ought to be dead, but I am fine. George? Georgie?" Haltingly, the captain gained his knees and knelt over his brother.

Sir George Carmadie moaned. His hands went to his head, then, swiped at his eyes. His spectacles had vanished as completely as the witch, the tower, and Miss Rachel Garden. With Wiggens' help, he sat up slowly upon the grass and blinked and stared about him. "Jeremy? Wiggens?"

"We are here, George," murmured Captain Carmadie, taking his brother's hand.

"Where? Where are you? I feel you holding my hand, Jeremy, but I cannot see you. I cannot see you at all."

The flat on Little Charles Street had never known such a crowd as gathered in its front parlor the following afternoon. Viscount and Viscountess Carmadie occupied the brocade sopha, which was the most solid of their youngest son's furniture, while Captain Carmadie rested somewhat comfortably upon the chaise longue. Tess sat upon an ottoman beside him. Ned Carmadie paced the chamber, while Michael stood with his arm resting along the fireplace mantel and Peter took up the wing chair, his wife Rebecca choosing to sit upon a footstool at his feet.

"Tell me once again what happened, Jeremy," murmured the viscount. "Even now I do not think that I have got it aright."

"But you have, Father. You simply refuse to accept it. I did think it a great bouncer when Georgie first explained it to me. But he was so certain of it all. And by Jove if all he said did not prove to be true."

"But a witch," mumbled Ned, ceasing to pace for a moment and running a hand through his dark curls. "There are no such things as witches."

"Yes, there are," insisted Tess.

"You ought not to have brought the babe, Mama,"

sighed Michael Carmadie. "She cannot for a moment understand what has happened to George or what is going on."

"Your sister understands all, Michael," the viscountess replied. "It is Tess and Jeremy who know the truth of the matter and the rest of you who are determined to remain in the dark."

"But a witch, Mama?" offered Peter.

"Surely not," declared Rebecca with a shake of her head. "This belief in witches is some eccentricity that George has acquired because of his sorrow over that wretched Ariel Browne."

"No, it is not, Rebecca," insisted the captain. "There *was* a tower with a young lady locked up inside of it, and I have got the bruises to prove that the tower was solid, too."

"You were in the midst of climbing up the thing to help your brother and the entire tower disappeared?" murmured the viscount, almost to himself, puzzling over it. "And the witch and the young lady, this Miss Rachel Garden, they both disappeared as well?"

"Indeed. And the witch is called Eustacia Nightwing, George tells me, and is the aunt of Miss Guinevere Longfellow who is Lord Margate's intended."

"Guinevere's Aunt Eustacia!" cried Rebecca, astounded. "A witch? Oh, Jeremy, that is truly absurd. Why, Peter and I have been to any number of entertainments which Lord Margate and Guinevere have attended and Eustacia Nightwing is always with them. There is nothing witchlike about the woman. She is a most retiring little soul with flaming red hair and the most shocking sense of fashion."

"Who keeps a young lady locked in a magical tower

and has blinded Georgie," finished Captain Jeremy Carmadie for her, growing most weary of his sister-in-law's doubts. I am growing weary of everyone's doubts, he thought grumpily. And I am exceeding sorry for the difficult time I gave George when he attempted to explain it to me, too. "Tell me, Rebecca," he asked gruffly, "did you attend Drury Lane last evening?"

"Yes, we did," replied Peter, hushing his wife. "And Miss Longfellow's Aunt Eustacia attended as well."

"And at midnight or thereabout, did she leave the theatre?"

Peter Carmadie thought back on the evening before. "Do you know, Jeremy, we all left the theatre about then. And I remember thinking it most odd that Lady Eustacia and Miss Longfellow drove off in their own carriage without even Margate in attendance."

"Ah ha!" declared Jeremy.

"Ah ha, what?" asked Rebecca. "Do you think, Jeremy, that because Guinevere and her aunt left the theatre when the play was over that it somehow proves that Miss Nightwing is a witch? Great heavens, you are as 'round about in your head as George."

"Enough, Rebecca," rumbled Viscount Carmadie's deep baritone. "Certainly it does not prove that the woman is a witch, but it does not disprove it either. And it is odd that they should not share Margate's carriage. Most odd."

"Horace?" the viscountess gazed at her husband and smiled the tiniest smile. "Does that mean that you believe what Jeremy has told us?"

The viscount sighed. "Well, something has happened to Georgie's eyesight. We shall know more, I expect, once Philips has finished with him. But something dire happened to the boy between last evening and this morning. And both Wiggens and Jeremy were with him. And both Wiggens and Jeremy tell the exact same story."

"Yes," nodded Michael, "and though we cannot prove that this Miss Eustacia Nightwing is a witch, apparently Rebecca and Peter do not know where the coach might have taken her after midnight. She might well have been in some magical tower with George and his Miss Garden. If there were such a thing as a magical tower and if we believed in witches."

"I believe in witches," declared Tess adamantly.

"And so do I now, my dear," agreed Jeremy, giving his little sister a pat on the head. "And if I know George, this bit of a setback with his eyes is not going to deter him from facing the old harpy again. He is determined to rescue Miss Garden and he will do it blind or not and whether we agree to help him or not."

The four Carmadie brothers searched each other's eyes and then studied their father's grim countenance.

"I expect the best thing will be for mama and Tess and Peter and Rebecca to remain in London with George while Michael and Ned and Jeremy and I divide up the countryside and search for Miss Garden," the viscount declared, abruptly. "Magical towers, witches, or not, the young woman is missing and George's happiness apparently depends upon locating her. Peter, you will be responsible for keeping George out of harm's way while we are gone, eh? And since you and Rebecca are both known to this Miss

Longfellow and her aunt, you shall become our spies. The presence of the two of you at the entertainments they attend will not seem at all suspicious. You will be in a position to keep a close watch upon them."

Peter nodded. "If Eustacia Nightwing remains with Miss Longfellow in London, Rebecca and I will cling to them like fleas. We will hop about after them wherever they go. And you must pay attention to their every word, Becca, so that we may let the others know of anything they say pertaining to Miss Rachel Garden," he added, tugging at a strand of his wife's hair. "You will do that for me, will you not, dearest?"

Rebecca nodded. "I think you are all quite as mad as George," she declared. "Eustacia Nightwing is not a witch. There are no such things as witches. But I will be dashed if I am going to sit about and do nothing, Peter, if that woman has somehow harmed George."

"And neither are Tess and I," agreed Lady Carmadie. "While Horace and the boys are scouring the countryside for word of Miss Garden, and Rebecca and Peter are staying close to Miss Longfellow and her aunt, Tess and I shall discover London most stimulating and flit about taking in all the sights, keeping our eyes open for anything that may help us to locate George's Miss Garden. I may be too old to recognize a beleaguered heroine or a magic tower, but Tess will know both at once, will you not, dear?"

# Chapter Six

Miss Rachel Garden stared vaguely down from her chamber window upon the sedate morning traffic of Laura Place. Her eyes brimmed with tears as they had for countless days now. It made not the least bit of difference that Guinevere had come to visit her for an entire week and had only departed yesterday. No difference at all. Guinevere was sweet and kind and had always been so. But Guinevere had not the least idea what had happened to Sir George and could not reassure Rachel in any way as to his present situation. She had, in fact, brought news that had driven Rachel even farther into the dismals. Not once since Aunt Eustacia had discovered Sir George and Rachel together and had banished Rachel to Bath, not once since then, had Sir George appeared at any of the London entertainments. Rumors raged in London, in fact, Guinevere had confided, that Sir George had attempted to put a period to his life on the very evening of Miss Ariel Browne's marriage to Lord Blanchard. For that was the very evening, she had said, that Aunt Eustacia had discovered them together and he had disappeared from Society.

"Oh, George," Rachel sighed, gulping back her

tears. "It is all of it my fault. Whatever Aunt Eustacia has done to you, it is all my fault. I ought never once to have lowered my hair to you and invited you up into the tower."

But it was much too late for such self-recriminations. Rachel knew that well enough. Sitting behind a window and blinking back tears would do nothing to save her George. And it was clear that he required saving. Never would he have gone into seclusion if Aunt Eustacia had not done something dreadful to him. Rachel was positive of that. If Aunt Eustacia had not done something dreadful to him, he would even now be riding about the countryside in search of her.

But perhaps he was riding about the countryside in search of her. Perhaps that was why no one in London had seen him since that dreadful night. Hope began to grow in Rachel's heart. He was her hero, after all. Aunt Glennis had seen him in her crystal ball years ago and had been certain that he was meant to be her hero. Rachel's tears began to lessen and her confidence began to grow. George would come for her. He must come for her. It was fated to be so. Aunt Glennis had said so and Aunt Glennis would never lie.

Sir George placed the spectacles upon his nose and stared hopefully in Wiggens' direction.

"Well?" asked his man hopefully.

"Better."

"Better? You can see me?"

"Yes. That is, I can make out the difference between yourself and the chair behind you, Wiggens, which is much better than any of the other spectacles I have tried."

"It is not a chair behind me, Sir George," murmured Wiggens despairingly. "It is a sopha."

"Oh. Well, but, I can still make you out, Wiggens, from the sopha. You are precisely there," he said, pointing. "And the sopha is there," he added, pointing again.

Wiggens' countenance brightened.

"Now, can you make me out from Wiggens?" asked a voice from the parlor threshold.

"Peter?"

"Indeed, Georgie, but you know that from my voice. Stay where you are and Wiggens and I shall shuffle ourselves like a deck of cards—well, two cards of a deck—eh, Wiggens?" And striding into the chamber, the eldest of the Carmadie brothers took a stand beside Wiggens, then switched sides, then switched back again. Then both gentlemen turned about in a circle and switched places several more times and then stood still.

"That is you, Peter," declared Sir George, pointing. "And that is Wiggens. And that is my sopha."

"Well," sighed Wiggens dejectedly, "you are correct on one point, sir. That *is* your sopha."

Sir George disengaged himself from the grip of the chaise longue and stepped carefully toward the two. He came to a stop directly before Wiggens' nose and peered intently at him through the spectacles. "Wiggens," he pronounced and then took one step sideways. "Peter."

"Correct now, but how much of us do you see, Georgie?" asked his brother quietly.

"Well, I can see your faces, but they are all muzzy sort of."

"Muzzy?"

"You know, Peter, sort of misty and fuzzy all at once. But I can see you both."

"I shall make tea, shall I, sir?" asked Wiggens.

"Would you like tea, Peter?" Sir George asked.

"Love some," nodded his brother.

"You are nodding! I can see that!"

Wiggens took himself off to the little kitchen and Peter took his brother's arm and led him to the sopha where he took a seat beside him. "I know you are anxious to be off in search of Miss Garden, George, but you cannot go riding about the countryside when you cannot see any better than you can now."

"The horse can see."

"And will the horse recognize Miss Garden if he should come upon her?"

"Well, no. But I will know her, Peter. I do not need eyes to recognize the woman I love. The feel of her, the smell of her, the sound of her voice are all most familiar to me."

"And if she remains in this tower that you and Jeremy speak of? You will never be near enough to feel her or smell her."

"But I will hear her."

"Not if she does not realize that you are there and so does not speak. No, it is useless, George, for you to attempt to discover the lady's whereabouts in such a condition. I will speak to Philips again. He says he cannot make any stronger lenses, but perhaps I can persuade him to attempt it. He did not think he could make these, after all, but he did. No,

George, do not look so dejected. We are all of us searching for Miss Rachel Garden. We will discover her whereabouts, I promise you. Witch or no witch, tower or no tower, one of us will find the lady. Jeremy has gone so far as to borrow Lord Margate's yacht. We received a letter from him only this morning. He has already got as far as Liverpool and he vows he will sail straight up past Scotland and into the North Atlantic and back down into the North Sea if he must. And Father has ridden south and Michael west, and Ned has set himself the task of scouring all of northeast England."

"It will take forever," sighed Sir George. "And it is not right. I am the one ought to be searching, not all of them."

"But you cannot at the moment, George, and they can. As soon as you can see, my lad, you and I will set off together, eh? Oh, and Miss Longfellow and her Aunt Eustacia have returned to London. They were absent, you know, for a week or so. But only last evening they both attended the opera with Margate. Rebecca spoke to them and asked after Miss Garden. Miss Longfellow, Becca said, appeared to wish to speak about her cousin but was prevented from doing so by her aunt. Rebecca believes there is something havey-cavey going on now, George, and she is with us in full. My darling girl's suspicions are on the upsweep and she is determined to beat us all out by discovering Miss Garden's whereabouts on her own. She believes that wherever Miss Longfellow and her aunt went when they left London, it was to visit Miss Garden. In fact, Becca says she is certain of it. And she is determined to get Miss Longfellow alone so that she may ask her for Miss Garden's present direction without fear that Miss Nightwing will interrupt and prevent it.

At ten o'clock on the following Tuesday, Miss Guinevere Longfellow stared across the Severs' drawing room and her jaw dropped. She stood up immediately and took possession of Lord Margate's arm and whispered in his ear. Lord Margate's gaze fell questioningly upon her but he merely nodded. Pardoning himself from the group with whom they conversed, he escorted Miss Longfellow across the Turkish carpeting to a set of French doors which stood open and led onto a tiny balcony. "Sir George?" he called quietly as he strolled outside with his lady upon his arm.

"Y-yes. Is that you, Margate?"

"Indeed and I have Miss Longfellow with me."

"You do?" Hesitantly, Sir George Carmadie, his hand clutching the balcony rail, made his way out of the shadows and into the light from the drawing room. "I hoped you would see me, Miss Longfellow, but I dared not remain in the light for very long because your aunt is here, is she not? Rebecca said that your aunt would be here."

"Yes, she is," murmured Miss Longfellow, "but she cannot see you now because Beryl and I are standing in her way. Oh, you poor man! How could Aunt Eustacia have done such a cruel thing! Can you see me at all?"

"N-not very well," stuttered Sir George, nervously. "I—these are the strongest spectacles Peter could procure, but they are not very helpful. Good evening, Margate."

"Good evening, George. What did you mean, Guinevere, about your aunt being cruel?"

"Oh! Nothing! That is—"

"You merely meant that it was cruel of her to send Miss Garden out of my reach, did you not?" offered Sir George, divining from Margate's question and Miss Longfellow's indecision that his old schoolmate knew nothing of Eustacia's witchcraft.

Miss Longfellow gazed at Sir George with the most grateful eyes, but he could not actually see her eyes and did not realize.

"I have fallen in love with Miss Garden," he said in explanation, "and now she is gone."

"I know. I gave Jeremy the loan of my yacht to search for her. You are star-crossed in love, George," murmured Margate. "First Miss Browne and now Miss Garden."

"I realize," replied Sir George.

"Beryl, will you not go back and keep Aunt Eustacia occupied?" Miss Longfellow asked softly. "There is something I should very much like to discuss with Sir George and I do not wish my aunt to come looking for me."

Margate glanced from one to the other of them and then gave Miss Longfellow a kiss upon the cheek and departed. "I shall come back for you in five minutes," he said over his shoulder as he reentered the drawing room. "Take Sir George back into the shadows, Guinevere. Your Aunt Eustacia will see him else."

Miss Longfellow stepped forward and took Sir George's arm and escorted him to the side of the wide open French doors. "How do you come to be here?" she asked softly.

"Rebecca—Mrs. Carmadie—is my sister-in-law. She and Peter planned to attend, but she took ill and Peter would not leave her side. Rebecca said that you would be in attendance this evening. I thought, if I came myself, perhaps you would see fit to speak to me about Rachel."

"I have wished to speak to you about Rachel since first you danced with her all those weeks ago," sighed Miss Longfellow. "You are her knight. I recognized you at once. I cannot believe that Aunt Eustacia has been so evil as to make you blind!"

"I am not blind," declared Sir George. "I am merely—merely—a bit more nearsighted than once I was."

"Oh."

"Yes, and you must not pity me. It is all my own doing. I failed Rachel. If I had been more adept, I would have had her out of that tower before your aunt realized a thing. I forgot the scissors," he added sorrowfully. "What a ninny, to forget the scissors. Rachel would be free now, else. You are not a witch, too, are you?" he asked then. "I never thought—"

"Yes, well, I am a witch," Miss Longfellow replied. "I come from a long line of witches. But all witches are not like Aunt Eustacia. My mama is sweet and kind. It was she told Rachel years ago that you would appear to rescue her."

"She did? Your mama? Still, I expect you do not know where Rachel is now?"

"Not precisely. She was with my mama in Bath but there is no telling if she remains there. However, if I were in search of Rachel, I should definitely consult my mama upon the matter."

"You would?"

"Indeed, because she will know you are Rachel's knight directly she lays eyes upon you and, if you impress her as a proper young gentleman, she may be inclined to speak up for you to Aunt Eustacia which will save you an enormous amount of trouble. Mama is Aunt Eustacia's elder sister."

"Oh," murmured Sir George. "And if I do not impress your mama as a proper young gentleman?"

"I expect she will turn you into a toad."

"What is her name, your mama?"

"Why, it is Longfellow, the same as mine. Mrs. Glennis Longfellow. If you truly love Rachel, Sir George, you will seek Mama out in Bath. And that is all I can tell you. Beryl is returning and I must go in a moment. How did you get to this balcony? I did not see you enter the drawing room."

"No, I came up the outside steps."

"Can you get back down them by yourself?" asked Miss Longfellow. "I mean, you will not slip and break your neck?"

"I shall do nicely," Sir George lied. He had taken four missteps on the ascent earlier and his shins and knees were sorely bruised. But he did not like to request Miss Longfellow or Margate to lend him aid in descending. If either were gone from Eustacia Nightwing's sight for too long a time, she might well suspect something and come onto the balcony in search of them.

"Do you mean to tell me, Wiggens, that you have not the least idea where he has gone?" cried Sir George's mama. "How could you allow him to go

out at all? It is the middle of the night and he cannot see, Wiggens. He cannot see one foot in front
of him. He will be killed!"

"Sshhh, Mama. It is hardly Wiggens' fault if
George has chosen to go off somewhere. Wiggens
is Georgie's man, not his keeper," murmured Peter
Carmadie. "Besides, I think I know where he may
be. It is likely he went to the Severs' in Russell
Square. Rebecca told him that Miss Longfellow
would be there. And since I refused to go until I
knew Becca's condition to be not at all serious, it is
most likely that George went instead. He will have
thought to confront Miss Longfellow and her aunt
there. And George can see farther than a foot now,
Mama. Everything is blurry and misshapen, he says,
but he can see almost three feet in front of him with
his new spectacles."

"Oh my heavens!" cried his mama. "Three feet
in front of him and everything blurry and misshapen! He will be found dead in the gutter, mark
my words!"


Sir George sat for a long while upon the bottom
step of the Severs' balcony where he had come to
a bone-thudding halt after slipping wildly down the
stairs. He thought for the longest time that his heart
would shrivel up and die. How was he to get to Bath?
How could he get to Bath, when he could not even
get down a flight of stairs on his own? And if he did
not get to Bath, he stood not the least chance of
finding Rachel. He knew that now. Letters had arrived only this morning from all parts of the country.
Peter had refused to read them to him, saying only

that his father and his brothers were continuing to search, but Sir George knew what the letters said. He had known immediately from the way Wiggens had begun to tiptoe about and the way Peter had suddenly become quite jolly. None of the Carmadies had had the least bit of luck.

"And why should they?" Sir George muttered. "I am Rachel's knight. Even Miss Longfellow says so. Papa and Jeremy and Ned and Michael, none of them, would have seen the magical tower that night. And they cannot see it now, not without me to show it to them. If Rachel is in the tower," he added sadly. "Perhaps she is no longer even in the tower. Perhaps that witch has confined her to a cavern somewhere or stuffed her down into some hideous dungeon. And here I sit doing nothing!" he muttered angrily, and then gained his feet. "What sort of a hero am I? I must be off to Bath as quickly as possible."

With one hand upon the bricks and poking hesitantly with his cane before every step, Sir George made his way gingerly around from the rear of the Severs' establishment and out to the street. He raised one gloved hand and heard a coach pull up before him. "I cannot see well," he called up. "Are you a hackney?"

"Indeed, sir," answered the driver. "Are ye blind then? 'Ere, let me 'elp ye." And with that the man tied off his reins and climbed down to help Sir George into the coach. "Where be ye goin'?" he asked.

"To Bath," Sir George replied.

"Ye'll 'ave missed the mail and the stagecoaches, sir," offered the driver. "Will not one ner another leave Lunnon until mornin'. But ye can hire a yellow bounder at the Deviled Swan what will get ye ta Bath by the morrow."

"To the Deviled Swan then," nodded Sir George. "At once."

"Aye, sir," grinned the coachman, closing Sir George into the vehicle and mounting the box. "Ta the Deviled Swan."

# Chapter Seven

Sir George clung to the strap inside the yellow bounder and wondered if he had taken the correct action. It occurred to him that he ought to have waited until morning and claimed a place upon the Royal mail coach. Yellow bounders were notoriously unstable and slow as well. Though this particular vehicle did not feel slow. No. The way it jiggled and jolted and jounced, it felt as though it were traveling at a tremendous pace. But it was not and Sir George knew it was not. Despite the improvements upon the road it would take him a full day of traveling to reach Bath. Still, if he had waited for the mail, it was a certain thing that Wiggens or Peter would have discovered him and either forced him to return home or insisted upon accompanying him. "Which would not be the thing at all," he muttered to himself. "I cannot put either of them in danger. It was unconscionable of me to take Jeremy and Wiggens to the tower in the first place."

With a sigh, Sir George released the strap and slouched down into the corner of the vehicle, bracing himself with one boot against the opposite corner. The bounder was large enough to carry two passengers. Thankfully, he had this one to himself. "Ought

to have driven my own curricle," he murmured.
"Make it in half the time. Except I cannot see to drive
the deuced thing." With another sigh he nudged his
spectacles up further upon his nose and stared out
into the night. Black. Everything about him was
black. Not even the light of the stars reached him.

By the time the bounder came to a halt at the first
of the posting inns, every bone in Sir George's body
ached. He stepped cautiously out of the vehicle and
peered hopelessly around him. When one used a
bounder, one changed vehicles as well as horses, but
Sir George could not locate the bounder to which he
was meant to transfer. He could not, for that matter,
so much as locate the steps to the inn. Mortified, he
stood in the midst of the busy yard with horses stamp-
ing about him and mud spattering up at him and
hostlers shouting and dodging by him in a great
hurry to change the teams of the arriving vehicles.

"Stand away! Stand away!" bellowed a deep voice.
And then a strong hand clasped Sir George by the
arm and yanked him straight upward and across a
saddle bow. "What the devil is wrong wi' ye, lad? Be
ye blind, er be ye lookin' ta end yer life 'neath
m'horse's hooves?" roared the voice from above him
as Sir George was tossed back against a solid body
and then flung forward. He would have sailed over
the horse's head if the enormous hand that had
seized him did not grasp his jacket tightly to hold
him down. "Settle, Flame! Settle, you dratted old
donkey! Aye, there's m'girl. We ain't come ta fight
wi' the rest o' these beasts, m'darlin'. We come to git
us a bite ta eat, eh?"

Beneath Sir George the horse settled and moved
forward at a walk and in a moment the large hand was

lowering Sir George to the porch of the inn. What appeared to be a veritable giant dismounted in the lights that shone through the open inn door. Sir George peered upward at him with great concentration.

"B'gawd, ye *are* blind!" exclaimed the giant. "What the devil do ye be doin' in the middle of a yard filled wi' horses when ye kinnot see a thing?"

"I *can* see!" exclaimed Sir George, his embarrassment making him querulous. "I am not blind!"

"Ho no!" replied the giant, "not blind at all! What be the color o' me eyes, then, eh? Tell me that."

Sir George peered upward determinedly, biting his lower lip. "Well, I cannot tell you that. I cannot see your eyes precisely."

"No, and ye kinnot see m'horse either, kin ye?"

"Yes, I can."

"Ye kin? That's a reg'lar bouncer," laughed the giant. "I kinnot even see m'horse. They done took 'er inta the stable ta feed 'er an' wipe 'er down, lad."

"Well, it is some other horse I see then. Right there behind you," Sir George declared, pointing.

"That, m'lad," grinned the giant, turning to look and then turning back, "be two a ol' Grimstad's hostlers carryin' a trough between 'em. How come ye ta be wanderin' about wifout ye kin see where ye be goin'?" the giant queried, placing a hand the size of a hamhock upon Sir George's shoulder and steering him into the public room. "Ye'll 'ave a ale wif me, will ye not? Two!" he called to a busy old man scuttling about the chamber before Sir George could protest. " 'Ere, have ye a seat, lad. Have ye a seat." And without so much as a by-your-leave the man tugged an ancient padded chair up before the hearth and

shoved Sir George down into it. "Now, tell me how
do a reg'lar bit o' Quality come ta be on the Bath
road at this time o' night when he kinnot see so far
as the tip o' his nose?"

"Who are you?" Sir George asked instead.

"Me? I be naught but a poor farmer out fer a
evenin'."

"Do you have a name?"

"Aye, name's Samuel. Samuel Blackmon."

"Well, I should like to thank you, Mr. Blackmon,
for not allowing your horse to trample me into the
ground. I am Sir George Carmadie of London."

"Of Lunnon? Truly? Not o' somewheres else, up
ta Lunnon fer the Season?"

"No. I have always lived in London. But I am on
my way to Bath, and most assuredly there is a yellow
bounder waiting upon me in the yard. I wonder if
you would be kind enough to point me in the correct
direction?"

"I'll be takin' ye to it meself," declared Blackmon,
taking the two tankards of ale from old Grimstad's
hands and placing one into Carmadie's. "Sir George?
Be ye a baronet then?"

"No, I am merely a knight."

"A knight? Well, an' fancy me meeting up wif a
knight. An' fancy 'im bein' obligin' enuf ta be joinin'
me in a drink. If this ain't m'lucky night."

Sir George was about to comment upon luck when
a voice shouted from somewhere near the doorway.
"Run, Sam, Leland's bringin' Flame ta the rear. No!
Too late! Git down! Git down!" And then a pistol
roared, setting off a tremendous commotion in the
public room. Bodies flew in all directions at once seeking cover. Samuel Blackmon sprang from the chair

beside Sir George's, tugged a pistol from the pocket of the drab box coat he wore, spun around and fired back. Then he turned again, grabbed Sir George by the lapels of his jacket, pulled him to his feet and shoved him down behind the old padded chair.

"What the deuce is going on?" asked Sir George as another pistol shot sounded.

"I reckon mebbe I oughn't of stopped 'ere tanight," mumbled Blackmon, reloading his pistol. "But it were the queerest urge I had ta do it. Like I were meant ta do it. No, keep yer head down, lad. Keep yer head down. Ye kinnot see nothin' nohow."

"Is it more than one man after you?" asked Sir George.

"A whole blinkin' army," muttered Blackmon.

"Why?"

"Well, I reckon onaccounta I had the gall ta stan' up fer Lord Harry last evenin' when them black-guards thought ta stop 'is coach, er they be affer me fer practicin' m'profession."

"For farming?" asked Sir George, aghast.

"An, bless ye, lad! But sure an' ye kinnot see me. I be Black Sam the highwayman. Not that I'd be a robbin' of ye, mind ye. No, I don't rob no yellow bounders. Them as is forced ta ride the yellow bounders got themselfs trouble enuf wifout bein' robbed. Bless me, but I were thinkin' as 'ow we drove them blokes off last evenin', but it appears they be back an' have done brought Constable Beiley wif 'em. Damnation, but I got ta git ta Gardengrove quick-like an check on Lord Harry. Like as not, them as is firin' be wantin' me gaoled so as there'll be no un at the 'ouse ta help his lordship. I'll lay ye odds on it."

Sir George puzzled over the man's words for at

least a minute as another pistol fired, the ball thudding into the chair above their heads. Samuel Blackmon fired in return.

"A constable is firing upon you?" Sir George asked then.

"Naw, Constable Beiley don't be ownin' no pistol. That gang o' ruffians what the hag hired fer ta terrorize Lord Harry, they be firin'. Beiley, he jus' be wif 'em. I be a highwayman affer all. Leastways, I used ta be a highwayman until Lord Harry hired me on."

"When did Lord Harry hire you on?"

"Las evenin', which is why Beiley don' be knowin' as how I have changed m'ways. I misdoubt but Black Sam'll ever roam the roads about Salt Hill agin, now that Lord Harry 'as found use fer me. But I ain't 'ad time ta fade inta 'istory like."

"I see. But you are certain there is a constable with those who are firing upon us?"

"Aye."

"And is there another way out of this room?"

"A door b'hind o' us what leads ta a parlor what gots a door leads ta the hall an' then ta the kitchen an' the back door. That'll be where Leland got Flame awaitin', but I ain't goin' ta make it, I don't think. I am out of powder an' balls."

"Clutch me about the chest with one arm and point your pistol to my head, and we will both stand up," said Sir George.

"Whoa, lad! Do what?"

"You are taking me hostage. There is a constable. A constable will certainly frown upon those ruffians killing a Knight of the Garter just to capture a highwayman. Hold your fire!" shouted Sir George then.

"I am Sir George Carmadie of London and this villain has sworn to kill me if one more shot is fired at him!" And then Sir George jerked Samuel Blackmon's arm around his chest. "Point the pistol at my head now," he hissed. Blackmon did as he was told and both of them stood, Sir George effectively shielding the giant.

A great silence enveloped the inn.

"Please do not attempt to follow us," murmured Sir George into that silence. "I will be a dead man if you do. Send word to London. To Viscount Carmadie in Park Street. Tell him that his youngest son has been taken captive at—at—"

"Salt Hill," growled Blackmon. "And tell 'im that does he want ever ta see 'is lad alive again, 'e had best bring hisself an' 'is money ta Gardengrove. An' all o' ye 'ad best not come near the place wifout you got this Viscount Carmadie wif ye or this knight be a deadman!" And with that Samuel Blackmon came near to yanking Sir George off his feet as he backed toward the door into the private parlor while keeping his unloaded pistol pressed steadily against Sir George's temple.

"Oh dear, oh dear," murmured the little lady with soft auburn curls and wide-set hazel eyes as she paced the front parlor of the house in Laura Place. "Now what am I to do? I cannot possibly go to him myself. No, I cannot. He would be most upset to see me. But I cannot bear to know of his troubles and to do nothing at all to help him." With measured steps, Mrs. Glennis Longfellow trod the Turkish carpet, her hands clasped behind her back. From time to time she halted and stared down into a perfectly round globe that sat upon a spindly-legged table beside a maroon sopha. Then she would begin to pace again and mutter fretfully. And then a most brilliant idea occurred to her and, taking the globe into her hands, she stepped determinedly into the corridor and up the staircase to the second floor. Lifting her chin and squaring her shoulders, she knocked with one hand upon the sturdy oak door to Rachel's chamber. "Rachel, dearest, it is Aunt Glennis. I must speak with you."

"Come in, Aunt Glennis. I am merely reading," Rachel said, swinging the door inward and ushering the woman into her chamber. "Why, Aunt Glennis, is that not your crystal ball? I thought you had thrown that away long ago."

"No, dearest, I merely said that I had done so. I have kept it hidden away for the longest time," murmured Aunt Glennis distractedly, plunking herself, crystal ball in hand, down upon the edge of a faded red fainting couch. "I could never truly part with it. Never. It shows me everything."

"It does?" asked Rachel, settling beside the woman and smiling down at her.

"Yes. Everything. Eustacia has always hated my ball because it would never show her anything but clouds and fog. And she always made such a terrible fuss because I could see things and she could not, that at last I pretended to dispose of it. But I did not. I hid it beneath my bed. I never consult it when Eustacia is near."

"I will never betray you, Aunt Glennis," Rachel assured her.

"Oh, I know that you will not. You are the dearest little thing and always have been. I have loved you from the first day that Eustacia brought you home with her. You and Guinevere are the darlings of my life. And if it were not for the two of you, I am certain that I would be nothing now but a sad, lonely old woman living in a shoe somewhere."

"Sad and lonely and living in a shoe? Oh, I think not."

"Yes, yes I would. And to think that I have Eustacia to thank for the both of you. Why, if she had not found you abandoned in that dreadful sea-cave and brought you to me to care for as an infant, I should never have known you at all."

"She found me in a sea-cave?"

"Yes, dear, that is what she told me. Some poor woman had abandoned you there and you were only a few days old. Eustacia, of course, had not the first notion of how to care for an infant and so I cared for you until you began to toddle about in leading strings. Oh, how I missed you when she took you back to live with her. But why, of all things, she wished to keep you in that wretched tower of hers when you grew older—"

"But Aunt Eustacia told me that my papa had given me to her in return for stealing her rapunzel," Rachel interrupted, aghast.

"In return for—why would she say such a foolish thing?"

"Could it be that she lied to you, Aunt Glennis?"

"I do not think so. She must have been teasing you, my dear. Or you misunderstood her. No one would ever have stolen her rapunzel, Rachel. Eustacia has never had any rapunzel to steal."

"From her garden at the dower house."

"But she never lived in any dower house. No, and

she has never had a garden in all the years I have
known her and I have known her all my life."

"Oh, how cruel of her to tell me such a bouncer!"

"Sometimes Eustacia is cruel," nodded Mrs. Longfellow thoughtfully, "though I have always attempted
to see what is best in her. She is my sister after all.
And she does do nice things from time to time. I
should never have married Guinevere's father if Eustacia had not bullied me into it and so I should never
have had my Guin without her. I did not love Mr.
Longfellow."

"You did not?"

"No, never. But he was always kind to me and he
gave me Guinevere to love and so I cannot be sorry
that I married him. But that is neither here nor
there," added the lady on a tiny puff of breath.
"There is a favor I must ask of you, Rachel. There is
something you must do for me, for I cannot do it
and Guinevere remains in London. Harry is in terrible trouble. I have seen him in my ball and he is
shored up in his little house surrounded by difficulties and disasters. And there are pistols involved in
it."

"Harry?" Rachel stared at the elderly lady beside
her. "Who is Harry, Aunt Glennis?"

"Harry is the gentleman I truly love. I have loved
him since we were children. But he did not love me,
I'm afraid. I thought he might, once, but it turned
out that he did not." Rachel's Aunt Glennis stared
up at her with a most tender look in her eyes. "He
married a very nice sort of young lady from Dover,
my Harry. She was an heiress by the name of Miss
Blankenhope. She is dead now."

"She is?"

"Yes. Died in childbirth, the poor thing, and the child with her, Eustacia told me, though I did never hear of it from Harry. I thought I would," added Aunt Glennis sorrowfully. "I thought that Harry might write to me of it, but he never did. I expect he thought I would not care a fribble about it."

"But you do care," murmured Rachel. "I can see that you do."

"Oh, yes! I care about everything that has to do with Harry. That is why I wish you to go to him."

"To go to him?"

"Yes. I shall send you in my traveling coach with my finest horses in the traces."

"You have a traveling coach, Aunt Glennis?"

"Certainly. It was given me on my eighteenth birthday by my Uncle Solomon, Lord of the Winds. Eustacia was sooo envious. Of course, Uncle Solomon did present Eustacia with Handy on her coming of age. But as fine as Handy is, he is no match at all for my sweet ones. They will carry you swiftly and safely and without the least cause for alarm."

"And where must I go, Aunt?"

"To Harry's house near Salt Hill. It is called Gardengrove and stands to the east of the town in a park surrounded by Metcalfe's Wood. I shall tell my horses, dearest, and they will not miss it. And when you reach the place, you must give this wish box—oh, I have forgot to bring the box! Never mind, I will fetch it when you fetch your wrap. You must give the box into Harry's hands and tell him to wish upon it carefully and wisely and all will be well with him. That is, if you consent to go."

"Well, of course I will go, Aunt Glennis. How could you think that I would not? And perhaps—perhaps

when I have delivered the wish box—you will look
into your crystal ball for me and tell me how fares
the gentleman I love and what I must do to be with
him."

"You are in love?" asked Aunt Glennis in surprise.
"However did you come to fall in love? Oh! Rachel!
Your knight has discovered you! I knew he would! Is
that why you have come to visit?" added the tiny lady
in surprise. "I did wonder why Eustacia at last permitted you to be free of that dreadful tower and to
come to me instead. Did he—did he attempt to rescue you and failed?"

Rachel nodded. "He came to rescue me twice and
he would not have failed the second time, if only I
had thought to hide the scissors. But I forgot all
about them, and Aunt Eustacia discovered them and
she knew at once that he had been there. She lay in
wait for him when he returned and oh, Aunt Glennis,
no one has seen my dear Sir George since."

"Well, if that is not the outside of enough! If Eustacia were not my sister, I should lose all patience
with her. Perhaps, Rachel, if you were to use my wish
box—but no, you cannot. There is but one wish left
in it and it must be Harry's, for I can help him in no
other way. But I shall consult my crystal ball on your
behalf while you are gone to Harry's, and I shall have
news of your knight waiting for you upon your return.
It will take a bit of doing, for the ball is most usually
concerned only with myself, but I shall find him for
you, dearest, and tell you how he fares and think what
he must do to win you."

# Chapter Eight

Lord Harry flinched as the last unbroken window at Gardengrove burst inward upon him, showering him with glass. He lifted his head above the sill and peered out into the darkness. He thoroughly expected to see any number of men swarming toward the house, all of them armed, all of them dangerous, but he saw no one, merely the moonlight beaming down from the heavens and glistening upon the park. He gave a frustrated sigh.

"How does she do it? And what the devil has brought her down upon me?" he wondered aloud. "I have not so much as thought of Eustacia Nightwing in years, and then one day she descends upon me and begins a battle to drive me from my home." Then he heard a horse pounding at the gallop along the graveled drive and his heart rose. That would be Samuel. He peered above the sill once again and spied one horse with two men upon its back racing neck-or-nothing toward the house. "Two?" he murmured, lowering his head and scuttling across the floor until he was out of range of the windows. "Two on one mount? Something untoward has happened again. Damnation! If one more thing goes wrong,

Eustacia will have Gardengrove before the night is out!"

Rising, Collier rushed from the front parlor into the vestibule and, upon hearing the horse come to a stop, he sprung open the locks upon the door and pulled it wide and in a moment Samuel Blackmon was racing toward him dragging a slender young gentleman by the arm.

Harry Collier slammed the door behind them, then stared at them in the light of a candelabra. "Who the deuce is that, Samuel?" he asked with a frown. "And what is he doing here?"

"This be Sir George Carmadie, Lord Harry. Lad saved me hide at the Tin an' Pucker. The hag's ruffians follered me there. Had Constable Beiley with 'em, too. Firin' off pistols they was an' the constable not doin' a thin' about it neither. If I hadn't abducted the lad, I'd be in gaol this minit."

"Abducted him? You abducted him, Samuel?"

"Aye, but 'twere 'is own idea."

"It appeared to be the only way to get Mr. Blackmon out of that inn," offered Sir George quietly, squinting behind his spectacles in an attempt to bring Lord Harry Collier into focus. "Samuel thought that you would be under siege here."

Lord Harry nodded. "Under siege and like to be dead by morning, because I will not give that witch Gardengrove. But besieged by the witch, I think, and not her men. I have not seen one man since the sun went down."

"Witch? What witch?" asked Sir George.

"Eustacia Nightwing," mumbled Lord Harry, leading the way to the summer parlor which lay next to Lord Harry's study upon the ground floor. "Keep well away from the windows—no, never mind. They are all broken now. I doubt we need fear any more glass flying about at us. Eustacia Nightwing is a true witch with magical powers, Sir George, who—" Lord Harry halted in the midst of picking up a brandy decanter. "You likely think me balmy, eh, believing in witches? But it is true. Everyone here abouts knows it to be true. And there are none of them brave enough to bring her wrath down upon themselves by helping me—except Samuel."

"I woulda comed sooner 'ad I knowed someun needed me," declared Blackmon. "But I din't know until las' evenin' when I comed upon them villains attackin' of yer coach. I ain't much good at ridin' the High Toby," Blackmon informed Sir George with a shrug as he lowered his bulk into a chair. "I 'ave gived away more profits than I 'ave kep', an' m'Molly be that fratched wif me fer it, too."

"Samuel is not only a highwayman, he is a philanthropist as well," Lord Harry murmured, handing Sir George a glass brimming with brandy. "Drink it, lad. You will need it before the night is up if you plan to remain here."

"Eustacia Nightwing," mumbled Sir George, considerably amazed. "Eustacia Nightwing is plaguing you."

"Indeed," grumbled Lord Harry, pacing toward the window. "She has already ruined my crops, poisoned my stock, caused my investments to go bad one by one and set a group of ruffians upon me. Though where they can be at this moment, I cannot guess. They cannot all have gone to the inn after Samuel, can they?"

"There were a goodly number of them," offered

Sir George. "It sounded as though there were a goodly number of them to me. How long have you known that Eustacia Nightwing is a witch?"

"You believe me?" asked Lord Harry, spinning about to gaze down at Sir George in awe. "No one has ever actually believed me before. Only the people from around Salt Hill. That is it!" he exclaimed abruptly. "All of the people here, townsfolk and farmers alike, are petrified at the thought of opposing Eustacia. That is why she wants Gardengrove, so that she can rule the entire countryside according to her own whims. Well, she will not have Gardengrove, not so long as there is a breath in my body."

"You have known her a long time?" asked Sir George again, setting the brandy aside untasted.

"For years," sighed Lord Harry. "She and Glennis were born upon my father's estate. At Nightshade Hill."

"You are Wesmorland?" Sir George sat up a deal straighter and peered up at the gentleman.

"No, my brother Sylvester is Duke of Wesmorland. I am merely a younger brother. But Gardengrove is all I have and I am damned if I will hand it over to the likes of Eustacia Nightwing."

No sooner had those words fallen from Lord Harry's lips than every bit of china about the room began to pop and shatter and crumble to the floor one after the other.

"Lord Harry be unner a spell-like," Samuel Blackmon sighed as Sir George attempted to see what was crashing around him. "I be willin' ta fight off the hag's ruffians all right, but I kinnot figure 'ow we be goin' ta fight off the hag 'erself."

"No, nor can I, Samuel," agreed Lord Harry. "But there must be a way. There must be."

The coach and four veritably flew over the road. Nestled comfortably inside the vehicle, Rachel very much doubted that either the horses' hooves or the coach's wheels ever once actually touched the ground. How splendid it was to be carried across country in such a remarkable fashion. Oh, Aunt Eustacia had poofled her here and there from time to time, and that was undoubtedly a much speedier mode of travel, but it was not nearly so elegant, nor so thrilling. In fact, being poofled was nothing at all. One was wherever one was meant to be before one even realized that one was going there. But this invigorating dash through the night, this was stimulating and vitalizing and most adventurous. Rachel rested her head against the squabs and dreamed of Sir George.

Once she had delivered Aunt Glennis' wish box to Lord Harry, she would be carried back to Bath in this very coach. And by that time, Aunt Glennis would have discovered what Aunt Eustacia had done to George and where George was and what must be done so that he might free her from Aunt Eustacia's spell. Thank goodness Aunt Glennis was not at all like Aunt Eustacia. Aunt Glennis was sweet and kind—so kind, in fact, that she had convinced Aunt Eustacia the very day Rachel had arrived in Bath to undo the spell upon Rachel's hair so that it was neither so long nor so heavy as to make her wandering about the town a troublesome problem. Now, Rachel sat comfortably in the coach in a traveling costume of russet and blue stripes with a straw bonnet perched saucily upon short curls as gold as guineas. She smiled a secret smile. "George will never recognize me," she murmured. "I shall be forced to introduce myself to him all over again."

Five tollgate keepers actually fled their posts in search of a bottle that night as Rachel's coach raced past. There was no coachman driving, no guard, no footman, not so much as a tiny tiger who blew up for the tolls. It was a startling sight to see, that vehicle, a sight that required a dose or two of spirits to ease the bewilderment it produced within one's brain. Never slowing, never stopping, the magical coach and four sped onward along the London-Bath road, glistening in the moonlight and leaving a trail of mystified gatekeepers in its wake.

"What the devil!" cried Lord Harry, diving for the floor as the chair in which he had been sitting rose into the air, soared across the room and thawacked into the far wall.

"What was that?" Sir George asked. "Collier? Is that you rolling about on the carpeting? What is going on? Is someone shooting at us again?"

"No, not shootin'," Samuel Blackmon responded shakily as the chair in which he sat began to wiggle and dance beneath him.

"Get out of it, Samuel!" Lord Harry exclaimed, gaining his feet. "Sir George, come with me at once. We are under attack."

"Well, I do not doubt that," sighed Sir George. "It will be Eustacia Nightwing, eh? What is she doing this time? Are you like to disappear, Lord Harry?"

"No, no, I have never disappeared. She is slamming chairs against the walls. Mine has gone down and Samuel's is flying across the room as we speak. Yours will be next, I expect."

"Hmph! As if I care," grumbled Sir George.

"Oh, you will care!" roared Eustacia Nightwing's voice from nowhere and everywhere. "You will all care! Frighten off my hired ruffians by pretending to hold a knight hostage, will you, Blackmon? I knew what the knight's name would be, when they came cowering to me. I knew! How do you come to be at Gardengrove, you ninnyhammer? Rapunzel is not at Gardengrove. She is in Bath! Bath! Did not Guinevere tell you as much? You are not merely blind as a bat, you are dumb as a doorknob as well!"

"Eustacia, come out where we can see you," demanded Lord Harry. "We know you are here now. You are not frightening any of us by remaining invisible."

"Balderdash!" Eustacia exclaimed. "You are all as frightened as little children this very moment."

"No, we are not!" declared Lord Harry vehemently. "I am not!" he corrected, deciding that perhaps he did not speak for Sir George and Blackmon. "I am frustrated is what I am, Eustacia, and if you do not present yourself immediately, I shall—"

"What? You shall what? You are grown into naught but an old farmer, Harry. I am grateful you did not wish to marry me! I thank the Fates each day that you did not wish to marry me!"

"Rubbish," muttered Lord Harry. "Go away if you will speak nothing but rubbish. I have no need of you to plague me more. Send your ruffians back here and let them try and see if they can shoot me through the heart before I send them one by one to their graves. I warn you, Eustacia, I will do exactly that."

"Yes, an' I will be a helpin' of 'im," bellowed Samuel Blackmon, gazing around him for some sight of the being to whom Lord Harry spoke. "Damned if I won't."

"I will help as well, and I do not give a fig if she shows herself or not," Sir George stated flatly, gaining his feet and feeling his way toward the sound of Lord Harry's voice. "Eustacia Nightwing is all flash and no substance at any rate. Might as well be invisible. Kept the young lady I love confined in a tower and then when I was about to rescue the girl, sent Rachel soaring off to Bath. What is there in that? Any chaperon in charge of a young lady who falls into awkward circumstances sends that young lady soaring off to Bath. It is not even original." Sir George at last found Lord Harry's arm and lay a hand upon it. "It is boring!" he shouted at the top of his lungs. "You, Eustacia Nightwing, are a dead bore!"

That produced a remarkably loud clap of thunder.

"Show herself any moment now," Sir George whispered to Lord Harry beneath the noise. "Where is Samuel?"

"Right 'ere aside ye," whispered Blackmon, placing a hand upon Sir George's shoulder as he gazed about in awe. "A true witch," he murmured. "Won't m'Molly have the twimbles when she 'ears this."


No sooner had the coach steps lowered themselves than Rachel stepped down them into the gravel drive and gazed about. It was not a large house, more a country manor than a mansion, and it lay under a great cloud. Rachel stared up at it in wonder. All across the drive and the park and the woods beyond, moonlight sparkled and glowed, but the house itself appeared steeped in darkness, a great black cloud whirling about it. Rachel took a deep breath, clutched her Aunt Glennis' wish box to her bosom and made her way to the front door. She looked about for a bellpull but there was none, nor did a knocker hang in the place where any knocker ought to hang.

"I expect it does not matter," she told herself quietly as thunder crashed around her. She made a fist of one daintily gloved hand and knocked upon the door as hard as she was able. She waited for a very long time, but no one came to answer. She knocked twice more and then tried the latch. The door sprung inward. There was a candelabra alight in the vestibule and lights flickering from a chamber farther down the corridor. Rachel took the candelabra in hand and strolled toward Lord Harry's summer parlor.

"I shall make a hedgehog of you with all your quills backwards so that you prick yourself to death!" bellowed a most familiar voice. Rachel halted upon the chamber threshold. "Better than that, I shall turn you into the ugliest of rats and confine you to Rachel's tower and she will screech and run each time she sees you. That will be a living death! That death will go on and on until you pray for me to end it! Boring am I? A dead bore?"

"Aunt Eustacia, you put him down at once!" cried Rachel. "At once, do you hear!"

Eustacia Nightwing, holding Sir George above her by the mere pointing of a finger while Lord Harry and Samuel Blackmon leaped fruitlessly up again and again to catch at his boots and pull him down, turned toward the young lady upon the threshold. "Rapunzel! What are you doing here?"

"I am come on an errand for Aunt Glennis," declared Rachel with an angry stamp of one foot. "Put George down at once."

"How dare you think to order me about!"

"I dare because I have had quite enough! You may do whatever you wish to me, but if you hurt my George, you shall regret it. I have Aunt Glennis' wish box right here, Aunt Eustacia, and if you do not put George down, I shall wish you to perdition!"

"Ha!" cried Eustacia, but Sir George did begin to descend slowly until at last Samuel Blackmon caught the toe of his boot and with a mighty tug sent himself and Sir George tumbling across the carpeting toward the hearth.

Lord Harry glared at Eustacia, then glanced at the young woman in the doorway. He gasped and took one step forward. Then he took a step back and stared at Rachel and gasped again. "Who are you?" he asked at last, his face pale and his hands trembling. "What is your name?"

"Her name is Rapunzel," cackled Eustacia, seizing Lord Harry's arm and pulling on it in glee. "Rapunzel! Rapunzel! Did you not tell me that night, Harry, to take all the rapunzel I wished and choke on it for all you cared?"

"That was the night my Annie died. You came pestering around begging to have the pick of the garden. Jawing and jawing at me like a thing possessed until I could abide it no longer. My Annie and my babe, Rachel, lay dying in the chamber above my head and you droned on and on about the pick of the garden."

" 'Take the blasted pick of the garden,' you said, Harry! 'Take the rapunzel and choke on it for all I care.' So I did! I did! I took the very best of Gardengrove! I took your daughter, Harry Collier. She ought to have been our daughter, but you would not have me, so I took her for myself!"

"My Rachel did not die with my Annie?"

"No, fool. My magic made you think it so. What a piddling little thing to make a houseful of people see a dead infant where one does not exist. Why it was far easier than the spell I wove to make you spurn my sister Glennis."

"Aunt Glennis," whispered Rachel most abruptly, her hands clutching the wish box. "Lord Harry, my Aunt Glennis sends you this box. There is one wish left in it and it is for you alone to make. You must choose carefully and wisely she said." And with quick steps Rachel crossed the carpeting and offered the box to Lord Harry, but he ignored it, allowing it to fall to the floor. He reached for Rachel instead, took her into his arms and hugged her to him.

"You are the very image of your mama," he managed on a gasp. "The very image. You are my little girl. My Rachel."

"Lord Harry, the box!" shouted Blackmon, gaining his feet. "The witch is going for the box!" The giant launched himself at Eustacia just as she seized the wish box and rose up into the air where she began to spin about, laughing. "One wish," she giggled. "One wish left! And it is mine! Mine! And only guess what I will wish, my dears, for all of you."

"Most likely something totally bizarre and without the least merit," drawled Sir George, picking himself up from the carpeting and making his way toward the blurry figure of the spinning Eustacia. "As terrible as my vision is, I can still see what a dull-witted old hag you are. Dull-witted and a dead bore to boot. I can see clearly enough to see that."

"You ignorant, myopic knight," bellowed Eustacia, ceasing to spin and coming down before him. "I wish I had made you totally blind. Oh! Oh!" she screeched as the box in her hands shivered and shook and a bright white light flashed from it.

The sheer force of the light sent Sir George skyrocketing across the room and crashing into the wall. He crumbled to the floor and lay still.

"Bastard! Villain!" screeched Eustacia. "You have made me waste it! You have made me waste my wish on the likes of you!"

"You have wasted more than a wish, Eustacia," declared another voice, and in an instant Glennis Longfellow was strolling into Lord Harry's summer parlor. "You have wasted eighteen years of my life and of Harry's life and of Rachel's life as well. Wove a spell to separate Harry and me, did you? Tried to get him to marry you instead, did you? How very clever you are. And all the time I thought that Harry did not love me. Yes, and I was so overcome by grief that I gave you free rein. But your reign is at an end now, my dear. Thank heaven that I discovered Sir George in my ball and saw what was happening here. I should have gone on believing all your lies else. Go away, Eustacia. Go to your tower or your rented town house or wherever you care to reside, but go now and never let me see your face again."

"Glennis, you cannot—"

"Go!" ordered Glennis Longfellow, pointing one long, tapered finger at her sister. And with a great rumble of thunder and a flash of lightning, Eustacia was gone.

"Let me go," sobbed Rachel then, pushing Lord Harry away and rushing to kneel beside Sir George, who was just beginning to wiggle upon the floor. "Oh, my darling George! You saved us all, my dearest. You did. Had she wished her wish we should all have been dead. Oh, George, are you all right?"

"No," muttered Sir George, reaching up until he touched her cheek. "I cannot see, my girl. I cannot see at all now. But it does not matter, Rachel. I shall always see you in my mind's eye as first I saw you, and I shall always smile at the sight."

Lord Harry took a step forward, but Glennis Longfellow tugged him back. Samuel Blackmon moved closer to the pair, but Glennis Longfellow shook her head.

"At least," sighed Sir George with a crooked little smile, "I shall not need to bother with these." And with a shaking hand he removed the thick-lensed spectacles and gave them into Rachel's hand. "You will keep them for me, eh? To remind me how much I hated being nearsighted?"

"Oh, George," sobbed Rachel on her knees beside him, and her tears came rushing down in torrents, raining upon him and wetting his brow and his cheeks and his chin—and his eyes. And Sir George blinked at the salty wetness of them. And he blinked again. And only inches above him he saw Rachel's face most clearly, and behind her he saw Lord Harry with an arm about Glennis Longfellow's waist. And to his left he recognized the man who must be Samuel Blackmon. With enormous enthusiasm, Sir George gained his own knees and tugged an astonished Rachel into his arms and gave her the most passionate kiss—smack upon her beautiful but salty lips.

"I can see you," he laughed once he had finished kissing her thoroughly. "I can see you, Rachel, and everything else, too. Your tears have made me see again and a deal better than before, let me tell you!"

"The tears of love are the strongest magic in all the world," sniffed Glennis Longfellow mistily. "They can undo any number of wrongs when they are true and come not merely from one's eyes, but from one's very soul."


That June the entire Carmadie family gathered merrily in the summer parlor of Gardengrove along with Lord Margate and Guinevere, Lady Margate, and Samuel and Molly Blackmon and Wiggens. A violin began to play, and as it did, Sir George and Rachel entered the chamber. Directly behind them Lord Harry and Glennis Longfellow entered as well. Smiling widely, the two couples marched to a spot before the long windows where the Reverend Mr. Able waited with an open prayer book and a grin. And Sir George and Rachel were married. And Lord Harry and Glennis were married. And Samuel Blackmon was placed in charge of Gardengrove until Lord Harry should return from his wedding trip. And absolutely everyone lived happily ever after—except Eustacia Nightwing, who slipped getting out of a hackney cab and fell in the gutter and broke her neck and never bothered anyone ever again.

## WATCH FOR THESE REGENCY ROMANCES

BREACH OF HONOR                    (0-8217-5111-5, $4.50)
by Phylis Warady

DeLACEY'S ANGEL                    (0-8217-4978-1, $3.99)
by Monique Ellis

A DECEPTIVE BEQUEST                (0-8217-5380-0, $4.50)
by Olivia Sumner

A RAKE'S FOLLY                     (0-8217-5007-0, $3.99)
by Claudette Williams

AN INDEPENDENT LADY                (0-8217-3347-8, $3.95)
by Lois Stewart

# LOOK FOR THESE REGENCY ROMANCES

# WATCH FOR THESE ZEBRA REGENCIES

LADY STEPHANIE                                    (0-8217-5341-X, $4.50)
by Jeanne Savery
Lady Stephanie Morris has only one true love: the family estate she
has managed ever since her mother died. But then Lord Anthony Rider
arrives on her estate, claiming he has plans for both the land and the
woman. Stephanie soon realizes she's fallen in love with a man whose
sensual caresses will plunge her into a world of peril and intrigue . . . a
man as dangerous as he is irresistible.

BRIGHTON BEAUTY                                   (0-8217-5340-1, $4.50)
by Marilyn Clay
Chelsea Grant, pretty and poor, naively takes school friend Alayna
Marchmont's place and spends a month in the country. The devastating
man had sailed from Honduras to claim his promised bride, Miss
Marchmont. An affair of the heart may lead to disaster . . . unless a
resourceful Brighton beauty finds a way to stop a masquerade and
keep a lord's love.

LORD DIABLO'S DEMISE                              (0-8217-5338-X, $4.50)
by Meg-Lynn Roberts
The sinfully handsome Lord Harry Glendower was a gambler and the
black sheep of his family. About to be forced into a marriage of convenience, the devilish fellow engineered his own demise, never having
dreamed that faking his death would lead him to the heavenly refuge
of spirited heiress Gwyn Morgan, the daughter of a physician.

A PERILOUS ATTRACTION                             (0-8217-5339-8, $4.50)
by Dawn Aldridge Poore
Alissa Morgan is stunned when a frantic passenger thrusts her baby
into Alissa's arms and flees, having heard rumors that a notorious
highwayman posed a threat to their coach. Handsome stranger Hugh
Sebastian secretly possesses the treasured necklace the highwayman
seeks and volunteers to pose as Alissa's husband to save her reputation.
With a lost baby and missing necklace in their care, the couple embarks
on a journey into peril—and passion.

*Available wherever paperbacks are sold, or order direct from the
Publisher. Send cover price plus 50¢ per copy for mailing and
handling to Kensington Publishing Corp., Consumer Orders,
or call (toll free) 888-345-BOOK, to place your order using
Mastercard or Visa. Residents of New York and Tennessee
must include sales tax. DO NOT SEND CASH.*

# ROMANCE FROM HANNAH HOWELL

MY VALIANT KNIGHT                 (0-8217-5186-7, $5.50/$6.50)
In 13th-century Scotland, a knight had to prove his loyalty to the King. Sir Gabel de Amalville sets out to crush the rebellious Mac-Nairn clan. To do so, he plans to seize Ainslee of Kengarvey, the daughter of Duggan MacNairn. It is not long before he realizes that she is more warrior than maid . . . and that he is passionately drawn to her sensual beauty.

ONLY FOR YOU                      (0-8217-4993-5, $4.99/$5.99)
The Scottish beauty, Saxan Honey Todd, gallops across the English countryside after Botolf, Earl of Regenford, whom she believes killed her twin brother. But when an enemy stalks him, they both flee and Botolf takes her to his castle feigning as his bride. They fight side by side to face the danger surrounding them and to establish a true love.

UNCONQUERED                       (0-8217-5417-3, $5.99/$7.50)
Eada of Pevensey gains possession of a mysterious box that leaves her with the gift of second sight. Now she can "see" the Norman invader coming to annex her lands. The reluctant soldier for William the Conqueror, Drogo de Toulon, is to seize the Pevensey lands, but is met with resistance by a woman who sets him afire. As war rages across England they find a bond that joins them body and soul.

WILD ROSES                        (0-8217-5677-X, $5.99/$7.50)
Ella Carson is sought by her vile uncle to return to Philadelphia so that he may swindle her inheritance. Harrigan Mahoney is the hired help determined to drag her from Wyoming. To dissuade him from leading them to her grudging relatives, Ella's last resort is to seduce him. When her scheme affects her own emotions, wild passion erupts between the two.

A TASTE OF FIRE                   (0-8217-5804-7, $5.99/$7.50)
A deathbed vow sends Antonie Ramirez to Texas searching for cattle rancher Royal Bancroft, to repay him for saving her family's life. Immediately, Royal saw that she had a wild, free spirit. He would have to let her ride with him and fight at his side for his land . . . as well as accept her as his flaming beloved.

## ROMANCE FROM JO BEVERLY

DANGEROUS JOY          (0-8217-5129-8, $5.99)

FORBIDDEN              (0-8217-4488-7, $4.99)

THE SHATTERED ROSE     (0-8217-5310-X, $5.99)

TEMPTING FORTUNE       (0-8217-4858-0, $4.99)